Praise for _____ _____

"*The Autumn Dead* and the beautifully moody and poignant *A Cry of Shadows* are as compelling and stylistically sophisticated as any detective stories I've ever read."

—Dean Koontz

"Well written, easygoing, and leavened with a bit of humor."

—*The New York Times*

"Slick and artful."

—*The Sunday Times* (London) on *Shadow Games*

"Shadowy and complex . . . First-rate."

—*San Francisco Chronicle* on *Murder on the Aisle*

"The poet of dark suspense."

—*The Bloomsbury Review*

"Gorman possesses the rare ability to examine real issues in a fictional setting without preaching."

—*Booklist* on *Dark Whispers and Other Stories*

"Gorman has a wonderful writing style."

—*San Francisco Examiner* on *The Autumn Dead*

"Interesting characters . . . a convincing plot . . . and a fine-tuned ear for veristic dialogue."

—*Kirkus Reviews* on *Several Deaths Later*

"Cynical, sardonic, witty."

—*Library Journal* on *Rough Cut*

Books by Ed Gorman

The Autumn Dead
Blood Game
Blood Moon
Cold Blue Midnight
A Cry of Shadows
The First Lady
The Marilyn Tapes
Murder on the Aisle
Night Kills
Night of Shadows
The Night Remembers
Rough Cut
Several Deaths Later
Shadow Games

STORY COLLECTIONS
Cages
Dark Whispers and Other Stories
The Face and Other Stories
Moonchasers and Other Stories
Prisoners

ANTHOLOGY
The World's Finest Mystery and Crime Stories: First Annual
Collection (editor)

BLOOD GAME

ED GORMAN

A TOM DOHERTY ASSOCIATES BOOK
NEW YORK

For Barb and Al Collins—the Beauty and the Best—
this homage to our friends Nolan and Quarry.

———————

BLOOD GAME

Copyright © 1989 by Edward Gorman

This book was originally published by M. Evans and Company, Inc.

A Forge Book
Published by Tom Doherty Associates, LLC
175 Fifth Avenue
New York, NY 10010

www.tor.com

Forge® is a registered trademark of Tom Doherty Associates, LLC.

ISBN 0-312-87748-X

First Forge Edition: June 2001

Printed in the United States of America

0 9 8 7 6 5 4 3 2 1

Chapter One

The boys were Mexican. They were about eighteen. Inside a rope ring each was stripped to the waist. Each wore snug brown leather gloves. They had ribs like hungry dogs'. The one boy had a decent left jab. The other boy had nothing at all. They had been sparring for half an hour in the sun. A dozen people stood in the small boxing camp in the alley of this midwestern town, and not one of them paid any attention to the two boys.

Guild sat on the edge of a rain barrel drinking lemonade and smoking a cigarette. A dog kept coming over with his wet black nose, and Guild kept petting him. In the sun Guild's hair was pure white, his eyes pure blue. The scar on his cleft chin had faded under his sunburn. He had spent the past three and a half weeks riding shotgun for one of the last stage lines in the Midwest. This was the summer of 1892, and as all the newspapers made note, the sun was merciless.

When one of the Mexican boys grunted and fell to the ground, Guild looked up and shook his head. He disliked boxing. He had once seen a redheaded kid go into convulsions, and ever since he'd had no stomach for the whole thing.

He would not have been here today if he wasn't, as usual, in need of money. The bounty-hunting business was going through one of its occasional lulls when the only criminals within five hundred miles seemed to be pimple-faced young clerks who had embezzled a few hundred dollars from mean employers. Having worked for his share of mean employers, Guild wished the pimple-faced young clerks well.

"You Guild?"

"Right."

"You come with me?"

"Sure."

The man wore a three-piece worsted suit far too heavy for the ninety-degree temperature. He carried a white surrender hand-kerchief in his hand and kept dabbing at his angular, pale face with it. He had nervous brown eyes. He wore a big navy Colt strapped in a creaking holster around his middle. The gun looked all wrong on him, like a pink garter on a nun.

They went in the rear entrance of the Northern Hotel and up a narrow flight of stairs, their boots making sharp rapping sounds on the wood.

They came out on the second-floor landing. The sunlight through the hall window was blinding white. In the center of it a hefty gray cat who looked capable of both stealth and wisdom rolled on his back in the light. Guild watched the cat as they continued their way down the hall. He reminded Guild of a cat he'd had during his married days.

When they came to room 246, the young man knocked three times with one knuckle. It almost appeared to be a code.

"Who is it?"

"Stephen."

"You're five goddamn minutes late."

"I'm sorry."

"When I say two o'clock, I mean two o'clock."

"Yes, sir."

"I don't mean two-oh-five."

"Yes, sir."

On the other side of the door, footsteps started coming toward them.

In a whisper, Stephen said, "That's my father. I'm sorry if that embarrassed you. He's just got one of those tempers is all."

Guild watched how the young man's right hand had begun to twitch. Stephen's face looked as if somebody had hit him very hard. He dabbed at his face again with the white handkerchief.

The door opened. A tall, stout man in a white shirt and tailored gray trousers and shiny black riding boots stood there. He held a drink of copper-colored bourbon in one hand and a dollar cigar in the other. His face looked fleshy but handsome. The expression he wore suggested he found the world had never quite lived up to his standards. Guild saw why a son of this man would be given to twitching.

"You're Guild?"

"Yes."

"Come in."

"Thank you."

"Oh. I'm Stoddard. John T. Stoddard."

He didn't offer to shake hands.

"You've heard of me?"

Guild nodded. "You're a boxing promoter."

"That's right, and a goddamned good one."

He said this with no irony. He said it, indeed, as a challenge.

"That's what I've heard," Guild said, as John T. Stoddard obviously expected him to say. When he was between good jobs like this, he did not mind on occasion eating a one-pound bag of shit. It was the two-pound bags that gave him problems.

Guild sat in a chair the color of dirty greenbacks. The room was heavily trimmed in mahogany. Deep maroon carpeting and white flocked drapes gave the place the feel of an expensive lawyer's office. John T. Stoddard sat in the center of a vast leather couch. He spread his arms out wide on either side of him. He gave the air of a potentate granting an interview with peasants.

"Did Stephen tell you about the job?"

"No."

"Good. He usually gets things wrong."

The cruelty of the remark caused Guild to look up at Stephen Stoddard. He stood to the right of the couch like a servant awaiting his next command. He refused to meet Guild's eyes, but Guild could see the faint pulsing twitch of his right arm.

"He does all right," Guild said to John T. Stoddard.

"I didn't bring you up here to talk about my son."

"All right."

"Do you know who Victor Sovich is?"

"Maybe."

"Are you being smart?"

"No."

"I don't like people being smart."

"I said 'maybe' because the name is familiar but I'm not sure who he is exactly." Now Guild felt like the young man. He wondered if his right arm, too, would begin to twitch.

"He's a boxer."

"Oh."

"Just about the best boxer in the United States."

"I see."

"You could show a little more goddamn enthusiasm."

"I guess I should tell you."

"Tell me what?"

"I don't much care for boxing."

"And just why not?"

"I don't like to see people do that to each other. You should only do it when you have to."

"I asked the sheriff here who would be good for this job, and he said there was a bounty hunter in town. I didn't expect a bounty hunter to be a nelly."

Guild flushed. A two-pound bag of fecal matter had just been pushed his way. He pushed it right back.

Guild stood up and said, "I want you to know something, Mr. Stoddard. In your small circle of friends and admirers, you're probably a very big deal. But you're nothing to me or most of the world. Do you understand that?"

Guild wanted to smash the man's face.

"It's just the way he is, Mr. Guild," Stephen Stoddard said. "He almost can't help it."

"Well, somebody better teach him to help it."

"I'm sorry I made that remark, Guild," John T. Stoddard said. "A lot of decent people are opposed to boxing. I probably would be myself if I didn't make so goddamn much money from it."

Stephen Stoddard gestured to his father. "You see, Mr. Guild. He isn't so bad."

"Right," Guild said. "He's a sugar baby."

"Please sit down, Mr. Guild. Please. My father really needs your help."

Guild looked at the young man and wondered why he acted so nice to a man who took every opportunity to berate and humiliate him.

Probably because he was curious, Leo Guild sat down.

John T. Stoddard gave Guild a cigar, and then Stephen Stoddard got them lemonade, and then John T. Stoddard started talking.

Chapter Two

The thing was, John T. Stoddard said, white people liked to see colored people get the hell kicked out of them. This was in general. While John T. Stoddard personally had nothing against colored people and had in fact supported the Union in the war, as a boxing promoter he would be foolish not to give the boxing public what it was looking for.

He used three examples. A year ago in San Francisco a kid named John L. Sullivan had fought a black man named Peter Jackson. The fight had gone sixty-one rounds. The crowd loved it. A month earlier a black man who was considered "the colored champion" had packed an arena when he'd fought Jake Kilrain. He'd lost to Kilrain. Then there was the business in Texas when a white man named O'Toole fought a mulatto named Waylou. The fight, according to one newspaper account John T. Stoddard read, had gone seventy-two rounds and ended only when Waylou's right eye popped out of its socket. Waylou stuffed it back in, but the referee, bowing to the outspoken demands of some Lutheran ladies who'd come to monitor the fight, called the fight over.

"My problem has been," John T. Stoddard said, "finding the right colored man to fight Victor."

"Victor Sovich?"

"Victor Sovich."

"And you've come up with a colored man?"

"Indeed I have, Mr. Guild. Or better yet, you call me John and I'll call you Leo."

John T. Stoddard smiled as if he'd just ceded the Louisiana Territory to Guild.

"If you've got the colored man, and the public wants to see a black man and a white man fight, I guess I don't understand what you need me for." Guild tried to call him "John," but it didn't work. He couldn't get the word to leave his mouth.

"The problem," John T. Stoddard said, "is Victor."

"Victor?"

"He's mad at me."

The way he said it, as if they were playmates in a spat, almost made Guild smile.

"Why is he mad at you?"

"That part doesn't matter, Leo. What matters is that we convince him to get back here in time for the fight Saturday afternoon."

"Where is he?"

"Across town."

"Doing what?"

"If I know Victor, he's soaking up the suds and spending all the time he can with Mexican women. He loves Mexican women, just before they go to fat. You understand?"

Guild nodded. "So what am I supposed to do?"

"Get him for me."

"How am I supposed to do that?"

"Take him this envelope. When he sees it, he'll come along."

"If it's so easy, why don't you do it?"

"Because he wouldn't even give me the chance to hand him the envelope. He'd just start swinging."

Stephen Stoddard said, "He's a genuine madman, Mr. Guild,

Victor is. A genuine madman. I once saw him knock a Brahma bull out with one punch."

"Great," Guild said, "and I'm supposed to go get him."

"The sheriff said that's the sort of thing you do," John T. Stoddard said.

"If you mean Sheriff Cardinelli," Guild said, "he only says things like that after about three or four schooners. He always gets sentimental and likes to talk about how tough all his former deputies are. I suppose it reflects on how well he trained us thirty years ago."

"You worked for him here?"

"No. Up in the territory. Near the border."

"Oh."

Guild sighed. "I'm not your man."

"What?" John T. Stoddard looked shocked.

"I'm fifty-five years old. I've got a crimped right knee from a riding accident, and I'm used to dealing with criminals, who most of the time are willing to have you bring them in because they're tired of running and hiding. Victor doesn't sound as if he'll be happy to see me at all."

"You're afraid of him, then?" John T. Stoddard said.

"Of course."

"I can't believe you're admitting this."

"Why wouldn't I admit it?"

"Well, because."

"Because as a bounty hunter I'm supposed to be big and strong and brave?"

"I guess something like that."

Guild stood up, fanned at his sweaty face with his Stetson. He was playing something of a game and he was about to see if all his theatrics were about to pay off. He had immediately sized up John T. Stoddard as a cheapskate, a man who would expect a man to accept whatever pittance he felt like paying. Obviously, there weren't many men in this town willing to deliver the envelope to Victor, whatever the fee. Guild figured he should get a good dollar.

"You're leaving?" John T. Stoddard said.

"I'm leaving."

"I'd think pride alone would make you take this job."

"Well, you'd be wrong."

Now John T. Stoddard stood. "How much do you think I was going to offer you?"

Guild considered a moment. He wanted to name a price that would establish a high ceiling. "Fifty dollars."

"Fifty dollars!" John T. Stoddard moved with the large, melodramatic motions of an opera star in his dying moments on stage. "Who would pay you fifty dollars just to deliver an envelope?"

"I wouldn't take fifty dollars, anyway. I'd want seventy-five."

"Seventy-five!"

Guild fanned himself some more with his hat and waited for what he sensed was the right moment and then turned to go.

"Do you realize how many young boys you're letting down?"

This one was so good Guild had to stop halfway to the door and turn around. "Beg pardon?"

"Young boys. In this town. Do you know how many of them have their hopes up to see Victor Sovich?" He paused and threw a wild hand toward the heavens. "Do you read magazines, Leo?"

"Sometimes."

"Have you ever read articles on how disappointment can stunt a young boy's mental development?"

"I see," Guild said. "If they don't see Victor on Saturday, they might be mentally stunted."

"You can scoff if you like, Leo. But that's exactly what we're dealing with here."

"Sixty-five dollars," Leo Guild said.

John T. Stoddard glared at Guild as if he were one of those socialists now stirring up labor trouble around the country. "You would put your own pocketbook above the well-being of eight-year-old boys?"

Guild shook his head. "Yeah, I guess that's the kind of low-down son of a bitch I really am."

Stephen Stoddard, whom Guild already liked anyway, had the good grace to laugh. At least until his father glared at him.

Chapter Three

He had sixty-five dollars' worth of John T. Stoddard's green-backs in his wallet, he was smoking one of John T. Stoddard's stogies, and he was sitting across the aisle in the streetcar from a very nice looking fortyish woman in a big picture hat. Her occasional glances at the six-foot Guild in his white boiled shirt, black suitcoat, black serge trousers, and black Texas boots said that he was probably a rapscallion, but an interesting one. Only when her soft brown gaze fell to the .44 strapped around his waist did her lips purse in that social disapproval city folks display for people not their kind.

In addition to watching the woman, Guild just enjoyed the ride. He liked the way the streetcar ran down the center of the sprawl-ing town with its three- and four-story buildings and all its bug-gies and rigs and wagons. He enjoyed watching all the men in straw boaters and high-buttoned suits and the women in flowered hats and twirling red and blue and yellow parasols, and he liked seeing all the big shiny store windows filled variously with high-button shoes and fresh bakery goods and pharmaceuticals and barbers in dark suit coats and handlebar mustaches stropping their razors and patting shaving cream on sagging faces. There was a music to the city that he sometimes longed for, the announcing clang of streetcars, the hoarse whistle of the factory changing shifts, the traffic policeman's street corner instructions to keep moving, keep moving, the sweet passing laughter of women he could at least dream about.

The woman he'd been playing eye games with got off about three blocks before he did, and as usual he felt a vast and personal disappointment, as if she'd been the woman he'd been meant to marry only she hadn't understood this and had gone shopping for rutabagas instead, and with not so much as a glance back at him. Not a glance.

The city changed abruptly. Where the stone and brick and wooden business buildings had given way to wide streets lined with forbidding iron gates and what passed for mansions in a midwestern town this size, so then did the mansions give way. Now the streets narrowed and the houses grew smaller and uglier in appearance, immigrant houses already sixty years old, older than the town's incorporation itself. Wild, filthy children ran the streets, and a cornucopia of garbage—the red of tomato rinds, the yellow of gutted squash, the tainted brown of sun-rotting fly-infested beef—filled curbstones and gutters alike.

Mothers bellowed harshly for their children, threatening enormous violence if the kids did not show their faces soon. Drunks wound and wove amid it all, one poor bastard puking into a garbage can, puking blood. There were cats and dogs and a few horses, all rib-gaunt and glassy-eyed from malnutrition, and here and there you saw a man smack a woman hard in the face or belly, and you saw a woman bash a man with a broom. White faces, black faces, brown faces, red faces, all showed the toil taken by living here. The sadness so easily became rage, and the rage so easily became despair. This was the part of city life Guild hated, the eternal poor and their eternal doom.

When he stepped off the platform of the streetcar, he took from the pocket of his coat the piece of paper John T. Stoddard had given him containing Victor Sovich's address.

The house stood two stories tall. It looked as though it had once been green. Now there was so much grime it was hard to tell what color it was. Not a single window remained intact. Cans, newspapers, pages of magazines, and plump brown dog turds covered the thin grass of the front yard. A small mulatto child, perhaps a year and a half, lay naked on the front step, fondling himself and crying.

A woman with a leaf-shaped paper fan bearing the name of a funeral home on its front side leaned in the doorway, watching Guild approach. Next to her squatted a dog with dirty white fur. From what he could see of the woman, she looked Mexican.

"Hello."

"What do you want?"

"I'm looking for a man named Victor Sovich."

"I don't know a man named like that."

Beneath the thin white cotton of her dusty dress, a beautiful, breathtaking set of breasts rose and fell with her breathing.

Guild sensed eyes watching him from all the windows of this tightly packed neighborhood. A word from her and two or three young men would no doubt appear, and Guild, if he wasn't quick and ruthless enough with his .44, would most likely be sorry.

"I have some money for him. Five hundred dollars."

He felt sorry for the quick, cheap light in her brown eyes. She had so little money, the child at her feet obviously malnourished, that mention of it made her almost ugly with desire. "Money you say?"

"Money. Five hundred dollars."

"For this Victor?"

"For Victor. Yes."

Guild would never be sure what happened next. No matter how many times he tried to reconstruct it, he just couldn't get the sequence straight.

Apparently Victor Sovich had been hiding in the vestibule right behind the woman. No other position would have allowed him to catapult out of the house. Or maybe he didn't catapult out of the house. Maybe Sovich came from behind him. Or from the side.

Not that it mattered.

The man with the fancy tattoos and the gray chest hair and the slick-shaven head and the biceps like coconuts started his attack by hitting Guild in the ribs.

Not that Sovich gave him a chance to do anything about it.

Before Guild's fists came up reflexively, Sovich hit him twice in the face and once more in the stomach.

Guild knew that he was bleeding, knew that he had peed his pants, and knew that he was making some kind of vague mewling sound.

Then Sovich slammed a right cross straight into Guild's crotch.

If Guild was not precisely unconscious at that point, he certainly was when his head slammed against the ground.

Chapter Four

"You keep this one there," the Mexican woman said twenty minutes later, bending into Guild's face with her soft breasts and her breath smelling of spicy Mexican food.

Guild lay on a red daybed in a white room. The hot sunlight shone directly on him through the room's single window. The room stank of food and tobacco smoke and heat. His head hurt and his jaw hurt, but neither hurt half so much as his groin. In the hallway outside, he could hear kids running up and down the wooden steps, screaming and laughing. One of them kept saying the dirtiest word Guild ever heard anybody say. The kid couldn't have been more than five.

"He lost his temper, Victor."

Guild tapped his sports coat. "He also took his money."

"You know what he did with the money?"

"What?"

"He burned it."

"What?"

He saw tears in her eyes. She shook her head in anger and a curious kind of fascination. "Look."

She showed him the white envelope John T. Stoddard had given him. She opened it up like an oyster. He peeked inside. Black curled ashes filled the white envelope.

"He is crazy sometimes."

"I'm sorry."

"He was cheated."

"Victor?"

She nodded. "I do not blame him for being mad."

"Who cheated him?"

"Stoddard."

"How much did he cheat him out of?"

"Many, many thousands. They have a—what is the word? Paper you sign?"

"Contract?"

"Yes. Contract. They have contract giving Victor half of everything. He gets nothing except five hundred dollars every three or four months. It is not fair."

"Where is Victor now?"

"He's in the kitchen."

Guild raised his head. He could never recall being hit so hard or so often without being able to swing back.

"What's he doing in the kitchen?"

"He's waiting for you."

"He wants to hit me again?"

"No. He only wants to talk."

"To me?"

"Yes."

Guild patted his right hip. His .44 was there. He drew it out and looked it over. "I'm taking this into the kitchen with me."

"He will understand. He knows how he can get."

"You tell him if he tries to hit me again, I'll kill him right on the spot."

She surprised him by smiling. "He scares you?" There was a certain pride in her voice.

"Absolutely. Now you go tell him."

She went away with her sweet, swaying breasts and long, good legs and bare, slapping feet. Guild sat up. He moaned several times and cursed. He checked his Ingram. He had been out for over half an hour. He focused his eyes. There was no evidence of concussion that he could tell. His groin was so painful, he was afraid to move.

The Mexican woman came back. "He asked if you would like a glass of beer."

"That would be nice, yes."

"He asked if you would like a cigarette."

"That would be nice, too." He paused. "Did you tell him what I said about killing him if he tries to hit me?"

"He is calm now. The only time you have to worry about Victor is when he is not calm."

Guild tried to stand up.

The undignified mewling sound came from his chest again.

The Mexican woman reached down and helped him stand. She put her arm around his shoulder and walked him across the sun-hot floor and down a small hallway past walls the kids had drawn circles and lines and sort of Aztec faces on with pencils.

The kitchen was a tiny room with a wobbly wooden table and four chairs and a stove and an icebox. It smelled of sour milk and beer and beans. Fat black flies squatted everywhere, the webs of their wings iridescent blue and green in the sunlight.

Victor sat naked to the waist behind the table. His shaven head was sleek and sweaty in the yellow daylight. From a bucket of beer he poured two glasses. He set one on the table for himself. The other one he shoved toward Guild.

"You'll be all right," Victor Sovich said.

"Thanks for the diagnosis, doctor."

"I've hit men a lot harder than I hit you, and they've been fine." He nodded to an empty chair. "You going to sit down?"

"The woman told you what I said?"

"About killing me?" He grinned.

"I'm glad you find it funny."

"Look, friend, your pride's been hurt. You'll get over it."

Guild knew there wasn't anything else to do. He sat down. He drank the beer. It was warm and cheap, with too much grain.

"How'd you get hooked up with John T.?" Victor Sovich said.

"The sheriff told him about me."

"The sheriff?"

"I'm a bounty hunter."

"Nice job."

"So is bashing people's heads in."

He laughed. "I guess you got me there, friend."

"You burned the money."

"Yeah, I burned the money, and I want you to tell John T. I burned the money. He won't believe it. He'll throw one of his goddamn fits. You wait and see."

"So you're not going to fight Saturday?"

"Sure I am."

"What?"

"Sure. We go through this in half the towns we're in. I walk off and he sends somebody after me and I beat that somebody up and then he agrees to pay me a certain amount up front before the fight. It's just a game."

Guild's groin sent pain all the way down into his ankles. "Some game."

"He's cheated hell out of me over the years. 'Expenses,' he'd always say. That's why there was always so little to split up at the end. Expenses, my ass. So last year I got smart. I started making him pay me my share up front." He had some beer. When he took the glass away he had a white foam mustache. It should have been comic. It just made him look meaner. "Tell him I want two thousand or nothing."

"That seems like a lot."

"It is a lot, but he's going to make a lot. I saw this colored kid. He's going to be good."

"You mean he's tough?"

"No, I mean he'll help me put on a good show. Didn't John T. tell you how it works?"

"Apparently not."

"The colored kids, they don't try to win. They can't win. They get paid by the round. They get paid for every round they stay on their legs. And they get paid more as the fight goes on." He smiled. "Of course John T. cheats them, too."

"How long do they usually last?"

"Five, six rounds. If they're lucky. Boy in Ohio went twenty rounds. He was a good one."

"He must have been a mess."

"Didn't John T. tell you that, either?"

"Tell me what?"

"About the boys I killed."

"Killed?"

"Yeah. He uses that in the advertising. How I've killed six boys in the last four years. It really gets the yokels worked up. You know how boxing fans are. A part of them wants to see a good clean fight, but another part of them wants to see somebody die." He shrugged meaty shoulders. "Anyway, this boy in Ohio, he went twenty rounds all right, but he was dead before they could get him out of the ring." He had some more beer. "The goddamn church groups went nuts, let me tell you. We had to leave town within two hours."

"You think you'll kill this new colored boy?"

He smiled again. "I take it you don't care for boxing."

"Not much."

"I won't kill him unless it just happens that way. I don't have much time for niggers, but I don't kill them on purpose, if that's what you mean." He stared at Guild. "You expected me to be dumb, didn't you?"

"I suppose."

"You're looking at the only boxer in the United States with a high school diploma."

"I'm impressed."

"You should be. Do you have a high school diploma?"

"No."

"I didn't think so."

"You want to know why I went into boxing instead of banking or something?"

"Why?"

"I enjoy killing people. Now, that may sound like a contradiction. Just a minute ago I said I don't kill people on purpose, and I don't. But when I *do* kill people, well, I can get away with it legally as long as it's in a ring. It gives me a certain kind of satisfaction. It really does."

A lot of tough guys like to tell you how tough they are. They like to sit over schooners for hours on end and tell you how tough they've been and how tough they are and how tough they're going to be in the future. With most of them it's bragging, because finally they're not tough at all. They just like to bully people with their words. But sometimes you meet a man who is truly tough, and he likes to tell you about it, too. Those are the ones you can't figure. They don't have to brag because you already believe them, but they brag anyway. Maybe they're just bored.

Victor Sovich was that way. After what he'd done to Guild, Guild had no doubt that the man was a genuine killer, nor any doubt even that he took pleasure in the killing. But this little speech was all sideshow barker horseshit, and Guild was sick of it and sick of Sovich.

Guild stood up. "I'll go tell Stoddard you burned the money."

"He'll throw a fit. You wait and see. A regular fit."

Guild snugged down his Stetson and started for the door.

Victor Sovich said, "You know something, Guild?"

"What's that?"

"I really think you would shoot me if I gave you half a chance."

Then he started laughing. The sound was loud and harsh in the small, sunny kitchen.

On his way out Guild passed the Mexican woman, who had been eavesdropping in the hallway.

Guild took her by the elbow and walked her to the door with him. "You owe it to your kids not to get mixed up with somebody like that. You understand me?"

She nodded. She had tears in her eyes. "I can't help it. I love him."

Guild shook his head and went on down the stairs.

Chapter Five

Stephen Stoddard stood in the open doorway. Guild pushed him out of the way and went straight across the room to the couch where John T. Stoddard sat so baronially.

Stoddard saw what was about to happen. He tried to climb backward up the couch, but it didn't work.

Guild shoved the barrel of the .44 directly into his face. From his shirt pocket he took a receipt and shoved this in Stoddard's face, too.

"What's this?" Stoddard said.

"What the doctor charged to look me over, you son of a bitch."

"You've got a temper, cowboy."

It was the wrong thing to say. Guild hit Stoddard hard enough in the mouth to cut his lip pretty badly. Thick red blood flowed from a pink wound on Stoddard's lower lip. He made the sort of mewling sound Guild had made earlier.

Peripherally Guild saw Stephen Stoddard move toward him. He had made a fist of his hand. It wasn't much of a hand to begin with and it sure as hell wasn't much of a fist.

"Please, kid," Guild said. "You're a nice boy. Let this be between your old man and me."

John T. Stoddard said, "He's right, Stephen. You go on down to the restaurant and have some dinner."

"But—"

"You go on now."

Guild had never heard Stoddard speak so softly or courteously to the young man.

Stephen Stoddard sighed and nodded. "You aren't going to hurt him anymore, are you, Mr. Guild?"

"Not unless he forces me to."

"He isn't so bad. He really isn't."

Guild's jaw set. "Kid, don't try and sell him to me, all right? You've got your opinions and I've got mine."

"You go on now, Stephen," John T. Stoddard said.

Stephen sighed again and left the room.

"You want a drink, Leo?"

"Don't call me Leo."

"It's all right if you call me John."

"I don't want to call you John, and I don't want you to call me Leo."

"You're one pissed-off man."

"He told me it was a game."

"Who told you what was a game?"

"Sovich told me that you and he do this sort of thing all the time. You hire somebody to get him back here, and sometimes he beats them up."

"Let me reassure you, this is no game. There's twenty thousand dollars at stake here on Saturday."

"Twenty thousand dollars?"

"You figure up all the wagers and that's just what you get."

"And how much do you make?"

"Are you going to put that goddamn gun away or what?"

Guild sighed. "You two deserve each other. You and Sovich. He tells me he killed some colored boys in the ring."

"Those things happen."

24

Guild wanted to hit him again, but he knew how Stoddard's son would get. The kid had plenty of grief already.

Guild waved the receipt at him again. "I want you to reimburse me for this right now, and then I never want you to bother me again. For anything. You understand that?"

"You're a strange man, Guild. No offense." Stoddard reached in his pocket. He paid in greenbacks.

A minute later Guild walked out. He slammed the door as hard as he could.

Chapter Six

Eating wasn't so easy. He ate a piece of steak that he had to cut up into tiny pieces, he ate American fries which he had to mash down, and he ate peas which were just fine. It was his jaw; it was sorer now than it had been six hours ago when he'd been hit.

He sat at a front window table of the Family Steak Restaurant, watching dusk bleed from the sky and the stars come out.

Nearer by, streetlights came on, lending the buildings wan light and deep shadows. People, mostly couples, strolled the business district, pointing out things in windows or simply standing on corners and taking in the air. You could smell rain coming, clear and clean and fine. The temperature had dropped fifteen degrees. After the heat today, the chill was a pure blessing.

Guild ate his custard and sipped his coffee. Because of cuts inside his mouth, he had to let the coffee cool, so he read the local paper, most especially "The City in Brief," which included such items as:

Ten businessmen were caught in a crap-shooting game last night.

Two young people eloped on bicycles from Oquawka, Illinois, and were married at Ottumwa.

Our compositors made Reverend Dr. Tilden's subject for yesterday morning read "Infidelity and Her Crown," when it should have read "Fidelity and Her Crown." (This struck Guild as very funny.)

Mr. Frank Redmond, a new baritone in our city, will sing at the Elks Minstrels tomorrow night.

Geo. Williams carries a full line of Blatz and Schlitz bottled beer for family use. Telephone No. 133.

Try a Turkish Bath at Ford's. You will like it.

Guild smoked a cigar with his second cup of coffee. Then he noticed the woman. She was one of those women it would be difficult not to notice.

She sat alone four tables away, gazing out the window. The first thing he noticed about her was how prim and pretty she was in her frilly, high-necked dress and sweet, angled little hat. He supposed she was forty or so. The second thing he noticed was the high, beautiful color of her skin. She was most likely a mulatto. In midwestern cities women who could "pass" were allowed to eat in white restaurants.

If she was aware of Guild's presence, she kept it a secret to herself.

Given the lingering pain in his jaw, he needed a distraction. She provided it. Like most lonely people, he speculated on the lives of strangers. What they did. What they wanted. Where they'd come from and where they were going. The trouble was, this woman being a mulatto, his usual line of speculation didn't work. Mulattos were especially despised. The only thing he could think she would want was to be left alone by men who wanted her carnally and by good citizens who wanted to express their contempt.

The hell of it was, that this woman with her dark eyes and full, exotic mouth did not look at all as if she needed Guild's understanding or pity. Indeed, there was even a certain haughtiness in the way she sat there, dismissing everyone who passed by with a disinterested glance, returning her gaze inevitably to the street and the clip-clop of fancy buggies and the first silver drops of rain sliding down the window.

Several times he started to go to her table and introduce himself, but he always stopped. He wasn't good at this sort of thing. His heart would get to hammering and his throat would twist into a snake of silence and his palms would get sweaty. He would stand there and everyone would stare at him and he would stand there some more and they would stare at him some more and finally he'd just sort of nod and leave, his face burning with embarrassment and his mind already flaying himself for his terrible performance.

When it came time for sex, he stuck to brothels. He didn't get crushes on whores; whores never broke his heart.

By this time, still sitting at his window table in the Family Steak Restaurant, Guild was reduced to little eye games. He'd pretend to be vastly interested in whatever was going on in the street. Then he'd kind of ease his gaze back to her, convinced that this time she'd be noticing him.

Only she never did notice him, of course.

And at 9:03, when he very slyly brought his gaze back around again to see if she was watching him, she was gone. He glimpsed her long, graceful back at the cash register, her sweet little hat floating just above the heads of the crowd at the front door, and then—

Gone.

He supposed he was being asinine, but loneliness was a burden sometimes and seemed especially a burden tonight.

He paid his bill and splurged on a fifty-cent cigar and went out to walk the streets. He could hear the vaudeville show over at the opera house, the harmonies of the popular ballads melancholy and irresistible.

Chapter Seven

He tried a whorehouse, but just standing downstairs in the vestibule convinced him. Whores couldn't help him tonight.

He did the second-best thing. He started at one end of a long city block and drank his way, beer-and-shot, beer-and-shot, to the other end of the block. There were nine saloons on that block. Nine of them.

In the morning when he awakened in the hotel, he found a plain white envelope on the stand next to the bed. The envelope depressed him. Not knowing where it had come from or what it contained reminded him that he'd been pretty bad last night. He did not drink liquor that often or that much, but when he did, and did so indulgently, the hangover always brought on memories of the little girl he'd shot and killed. Now he saw her six-year-old face and her patched gingham dress as she moved from the shadows of her cabin. By then it had been too late. He had already fired.

He looked at the way the dust motes glinted gold in the sunlight. He stared out the window at the hard blue sky until the little girl's face vanished. His bladder was full and his mouth was dry. His head pounded. Jesus, was he stupid.

He had just returned from the bathroom down the hall ten minutes later when the knock came.

He was dressed and already packing. He wanted to get out of this town. He had come here to try to earn some money, but instead he'd only met Stoddard and been beaten for his troubles. His bones still ached from the beating, but the hangover ached more.

He opened the door on the fifth knock. He jerked it open with some aggravation. He was not good at hangovers and tended to take them out on other people.

"You found the envelope, Mr. Guild?" Stephen Stoddard asked.

"How the hell did it get here?"

"I had the clerk bring it up last night."

"What is it?"

"You mean you haven't looked inside?"

"I'm too goddamned hung over for games, kid. What's in the envelope?"

"A hundred and fifty dollars."

"For what?"

"My father's money needs protection."

"You want to know what I think of your father, kid?"

"I'm willing to make it two hundred, Mr. Guild. For two days' work."

Even dehydrated and somewhat shaky, Guild thought the idea of two hundred dollars for two days' work sounded good.

"I need some breakfast," Guild said.

"They serve a very fine one here. I ate here yesterday. Toast and scrambled eggs and ham."

Guild smiled. "You sound like an ad in the newspaper." His stomach made noises. He'd done a lot of drinking last night but not enough eating. He went back, leaving Stephen Stoddard in the doorway, picked up the envelope, and said, "Let's go get some breakfast."

* * *

"I finally had to grab the shotgun and put it right to his face. I've seen Victor pretty mad before, but nothing like last night. Not even close, Mr. Guild."

"Will you do me a favor?"

"What?"

"Stop calling me Mr. Guild."

"Oh. Sure."

"Leo will do fine."

For the next few minutes Guild went back to his eggs over easy and his American fries and his two thick slices of ham.

Stephen Stoddard knew enough to just let him eat.

As he sipped his coffee, Guild said, "You really think Victor wanted to kill him?"

"Yes, he did."

"He just barged into your hotel room?"

"Just barged in."

"And ran over to your father and started hitting him?"

"Yes. And that's when I grabbed the rifle." He shook his head. "I put it right up against his cheek. I would have killed him, too, the way he was beating Dad."

Guild frowned and looked around the restaurant. It was beautifully decorated with flocked red wallpaper and gathered white drapes and mahogany appointments. Sunlight came in golden and warm through the front windows. Fancy men in three-piece suits sat talking to each other with great amounts of self-confidence. Women in big picture hats spoke more quietly.

"I believe Victor," Guild said, looking back at Stephen Stoddard.

"About what?"

"About your father cheating him."

Stephen Stoddard dropped his eyes. "My father doesn't cheat people."

"Sure he does, kid, and you know it." Guild realized how harsh he sounded. "I'm sorry I had to say that, but in case I decide to take your two hundred dollars I want you to know where I stand."

"I don't suppose it's important that you respect Dad, as long as you protect him."

Guild grinned. "I couldn't protect myself from Victor yesterday. What makes you think I can protect your father?"

"You'd kill Victor if he tried anything. I know you would. The sheriff told my dad all about you."

Whenever people said that to Guild, he wondered if they knew about the little girl. There were a lot of lies told about Guild in and out of the territory. Most of them had started over the death of the little girl.

Guild said, in a softer tone, "Why do you stay with him, kid? The way he treats you and all."

"You don't know anything about him." For the first time Stephen Stoddard sounded angry. For the first time Guild felt a little respect for the kid.

"Such as what?"

"Such as how he had to raise me after my mother ran off with a drummer ten years ago. Or how he was raised in the worst white slum in New York. Or how he was taken prisoner in the war and tortured by three Confederates.

Guild sighed. You could make a case for anybody. You could even make a case for Guild, a man who'd killed a six-year-old girl.

"I guess I was getting a little pompous there," Guild said.

Stephen Stoddard calmed down. "He really is a decent man. After all is said and done, I mean."

"He shouldn't have sent me over to Victor's."

"He really thought Victor would take the money and come back."

Guild asked him a question he'd been curious about since yesterday. "If Victor's so hot on the idea your father is cheating him, why doesn't he go to some other boxing promoter?"

In the strong sunlight, Stephen Stoddard blushed. "I'm not sure."

"You're lying, kid. Your father's got something on him, doesn't he?"

"Please don't ask me any more about that, Mr. Guild."

Guild stared down at the envelope between them. He could live four or five months on the money in there.

He told himself he had no right to judge John T. Stoddard. He couldn't figure out if he was just saying that to allow himself to take the money. As for Victor—Victor didn't scare him anymore. The kid was right. If Guild signed on, he'd be prepared to shoot the boxer. That was the only way he could be sure he'd survive the two days.

"So you're not going to tell me what your father's got on him?"

"No," Stephen Stoddard said softly. "No, I'm not."

Chapter Eight

At sight of Victor Sovich, Guild drew his .44 and aimed it directly at the boxer's middle. This was an hour after finishing breakfast with Stephen Stoddard.

Sovich, dressed in the type of black suit and white shirt and red-lined cape you would expect to see on an opera baritone, walked into the boxing camp smiling.

Guild, John T. Stoddard, and Stephen Stoddard all stood staring at him.

"You'd better tell Guild here that guns don't always frighten me," Sovich said, strolling up.

It was hot in the alley, just as it had been yesterday afternoon, though thunderheads had begun massing in the flat blue midwestern sky and there was a promise of a brief respite from the heat.

The two Mexican boys were in the rope ring again. They would precede Sovich and the black man. Guild just hoped the skinnier of the boys somehow learned to box between now and tomorrow afternoon.

A small group of reporters stood in the wide mouth of the alley, to the left of the livery stable, where you could smell heat and iron and smoke, talking to a small, prim group of churchwomen who were here to protest fisticuffs in general and any fight with Victor Sovich in particular.

"I wish I could turn you loose on them," John T. Stoddard said, nodding to the women.

"I wouldn't do it," Guild said. "I agree with them, remember?"

By now Sovich was directly in front of them.

Guild glanced up, sensing Stephen Stoddard's eyes on him. The kid could obviously sense what Guild was thinking.

Here was Sovich coming back to a partnership in which he was constantly cheated. Yesterday he had burned Stoddard's money. He had been through with the relationship. His presence here today could only mean that Stoddard had telephoned or sent a note—reminding Sovich that if money hadn't wooed him back, then maybe a certain memory would.

Guild wondered what Sovich had done.

John T. Stoddard said, "Victor, I don't expect any trouble between us. I've agreed to give you half the purse tomorrow. But I want Guild here to make sure that everything runs smoothly. I want tomorrow to be a good day for us."

"You just keep Guild out of my way," Sovich said, glaring at Guild.

"He'll be with me, Victor. That's the whole point of having him. But he won't bother you unless he needs to. Right, Guild?"

Guild felt as if he were stepping into the middle of an argument between two ten-year-olds.

"He'd better be damn good with that gun," Sovich said, "for his own sake."

"We'll have those boys take a rest," John T. Stoddard said, "and you can get in there and work out with Barney. I hope you didn't hit the bottle too hard last night."

"It wasn't the bottle," Sovich grinned. "It was the woman. Those goddamn hips of hers never stop."

Unlikely as it seemed, John T. Stoddard slid his arm around

Sovich's bear shoulders, and together they walked back to the two rooms in the livery stable used for dressing.

Halfway there, however, John T. turned around and nodded his head at Guild.

He wanted him to come along.

Given Sovich's power and temperament, that was probably a good idea.

John T. Stoddard hadn't been exaggerating. There was every possibility that Victor Sovich was the best fighter in the country.

His sparring partner, Barney, was a rangy man with red hair and small but astonishingly quick fists. Even Sovich had occasional trouble with the other man's speed.

But for the most part Sovich, dressed in black pants and black boots, had no trouble at all pounding Barney, dressed in black pants and red boots; no trouble at all.

The body blows were almost as impressive as the head shots, something you rarely saw. Twice Sovich hit Barney so hard in the ribs that he lifted the man off the canvas. He hit him so hard in the kidneys that he drove him to his knees.

After twenty minutes, both men were sleek and rancid with sweat.

The reporters had deserted the churchwomen and come over for a look at Sovich.

"Listen to how those goddamn punches sound when they land," said one reporter in a derby and checkered suit. "They sound like he's throwing bricks."

They fought for another twenty minutes until Barney's bleeding got bad, especially from the nose. He started choking on his own blood, and John T. Stoddard stepped in and said, "Why don't you quit now, Barney? We're going to need you again tomorrow."

For all his sweat, for all the redness in his face, Victor Sovich did not seem tired at all. Indeed, he seemed refreshed in some unimaginable way, as if punishing the other man so severely had made him younger, stronger, sharper.

When he stepped between the ropes, he looked up at Guild and said, "Remember yesterday afternoon, Guild? Remember how it felt?" He smiled. "Next time, you're going to look like Barney when I get through with you."

Guild hadn't realized until just now, looking at the boxer, what was really wrong with him.

Victor Sovich was insane.

Driving cattle, riding shotgun, serving as lawman, tracking bounty, Guild came across them occasionally, insane men. They weren't the laughing, sneering people he saw in melodramas. Usually it was just something in their eyes, some rage or grief that was frightening when he finally recognized it.

There was no grief in Sovich's dark eyes. Just rage.

He walked past Guild, back to the dressing room.

John T. Stoddard came up and stood next to Guild. "You stick right by me, you understand, Guild?"

"I understand."

"I hope you realize that the son of a bitch wants to kill us both."

Guild nodded. "Yeah, that's sort of what I was thinking."

John T. Stoddard shook his head. "I was going to take him along to see the colored man, but the hell with him. You and I will go."

From inside the livery you could hear Sovich yelling at one of the trainers. He really was crazy.

Chapter Nine

The town had a colored section adjacent to the mixed-race section. The buildings all seemed to lean at impossible angles, as if ready to collapse. You could smell cooking and heat and filth. A white policeman in a fancy blue uniform and a kepi-style hat walked up and down the street with a murderous-looking nightstick in his hand. Ragged children ran after him, trying to be nice. He wasn't nice back. He was just fat and Irish-looking and mean. The people here stared at Guild and John T. Stoddard with white, forlorn eyes out of black, forlorn faces.

Rooney was the name of the colored fighter. Unlike Sovich he did not have a training camp. He worked outside against another Negro in tufty grass behind a bar where an ancient Jamaican man played a squeeze box. There were maybe thirty black men in a circle around the two fighters. Some of them wore the bright clothes of the bayou they originally came from. Most wore the drab rags of stoop laborers. Most of them were drunk. The sparring served to take their minds off their problems. They sounded as if they had only one real concern in this world, and that was how good Rooney looked.

"Come on, Rooney, you take him out, hear?"

"Come on, Rooney, quit playin' and do the job."

"Come on, Rooney, show him your real punch."

Rooney was as squat and massive as Victor Sovich. He appeared to be a talented fighter capable of a good right hook and an even better left uppercut, but he did not have Sovich's skill at moving left and right as he threw his combinations. The other fighter pegged him several times with punches Rooney should have been able to avoid. Guild could imagine what Sovich would do to this man.

"He looks good, doesn't he?" Stoddard said.

"You know what Sovich will do to him."

"Sure. But Rooney here will put on a good show. You'd be surprised at how many people will bet on him. A lot of white people secretly believe that colored boxers are stronger. And that's what you have to play on—that belief."

It was then that Guild saw the woman start to draw something from her purse, something that glinted suspiciously in the sunlight.

"Shit," Guild said, and took off running to the other side of the crowd, where the woman stood.

John T. Stoddard shouted at Guild to stop, but Guild didn't slow down.

The men around here were too drunk and too involved in the fight to see what she was about to do.

Guild got her just as she was leveling the small revolver at Rooney's back.

He grabbed her wrist and tugged her free of the crowd. He must have grabbed her wrist very hard because she started crying almost immediately.

He pulled her inside the tavern. The place was shadowy and stank of the outhouse just outside the door.

"What the hell are you trying to do?" Guild said.

She just kept crying.

The bartender eased over for a better look at the two of them. Obviously he thought Guild had smacked her around some.

"I wanted to kill him," she said.

This was the beautiful mulatto woman he had seen last night in the restaurant. She wore the same sort of frilly white lace at her neck, but today her dress was of blue silk and her small angled hat of a darker blue silk. She was still beautiful, but Guild's impression of her fragile nature had been altered somewhat by the fact that she had just tried to kill a man.

"I know you wanted to kill him," Guild said. "What I want to know is why."

She glanced up at the bartender, who was still eavesdropping. "I don't want to talk with him listening."

"Let's go for a walk, then."

"Why are you so interested?"

"You wouldn't be interested in a woman who pulls out a gun and almost shoots a man?"

She sighed. "I suppose I would be."

They left a few minutes later. The bartender looked disappointed he hadn't gotten to hear what happened.

Guild knew he should be back with Stoddard, but instead he walked with the mulatto woman. Several times she tried to walk away from him. Each time, he grabbed her elbow and jerked her back. "What's going on here?" Guild would ask. "What's shooting Rooney all about?" But she'd say nothing.

They walked out of the colored section to a park where children splashed chill silver water in a marble pool and where nurses pushed strollers. Dogs yipped and jumped at balloons and a three-year-old got chocolate all over her face.

When they reached the river, he pulled her into a tavern where the bar was nothing more than rough planks. The place smelled of heat and hops and wine and vomit. He could see she hated it in here. The men filled their ignorant eyes with her.

After two beers—his, not hers; she wouldn't drink—he took her out behind the place and threw her up hard against a shed.

"I'm going to slap you," he said, "if you don't talk."

She didn't talk, and he slapped her very hard.

She immediately started sobbing.

"My name is Clarise Watson. I'm from Chicago. Rooney killed my brother a year ago."

"In the ring?"

"Supposedly."

"What's that mean?"

"It means that he put poison in my brother's drinking water right before the fight. It made my brother very groggy. He couldn't defend himself. He died right in the ring."

He could see she was fighting tears again.

They had been walking once more, back to the colored section.

The block they were on was filled with children and teenagers. The latter stared long and hard at the beautiful mulatto woman. Guild could not quite tell if they liked her or despised her. Their stares seemed to convey both feelings.

The sunlight showed her skin to be a beautiful coffee color. In the daylight her features were even more beautiful. Only the lines in her neck betrayed her age. She had to be nearly forty.

"I'm sorry I keep crying."

"Nothing to be sorry for."

"I loved him."

"I'm sure you did. You sure about the poison?"

"One of Rooney's trainers admitted it to me."

He looked at her closely. "He admitted it?"

She smiled without pleasure. "I had to help him. I gave him some bourbon and then I gave him myself."

"I see."

"You don't sound as if you approve."

"I don't."

"I wanted to know the truth."

"You probably could have figured out another way."

"Could I?"

They walked another quarter block in silence. Guild felt jealous. It was ridiculous, feeling jealous. Then he felt ashamed. He realized then that he was still hung over.

He stopped and turned her toward him. "You going to try it again?"

"I don't know. I've waited so long for today—built up to it so much. And then right at the last second you stopped me and—"

"I'm going to turn you over to the law. You tried to kill a man."

"What?"

"You're not giving me any choice."

"You've got my gun."

"You can always buy another one."

"Maybe I won't try. Maybe coming this close was good enough."

"'Maybe' isn't something I can count on."

"Do you have a brother, Mr. Guild?"

"I had two of them. They both died in the war."

"I'm sorry."

He took a cigarette from his shirt pocket and lighted it up. The smoke tasted nutty in his throat and felt soft and blue in his lungs.

"I'm going to ask you again. You going to try to shoot him?"

She made a face. "I suppose not."

"You're a hell of a lot of help."

She laughed. She had a wonderful laugh. "I don't suppose I am, am I?"

"You staying anyplace special?"

"The Carleton Arms. The manager is out of town. The desk clerk said I could stay till the manager gets back. He hates Negroes."

"Why don't you meet me tonight in the Carleton dining room?"

She looked at him carefully. "What are you after, Mr. Guild?"

"I'm not sure yet."

"I guess that's fair enough."

He paused. "Rooney wouldn't be worth hanging for."

"Did you ever get over the death of your brothers?"

"Not really."

"Then you know what I'm going through, Mr. Guild."

With that, she walked off, making it clear that she didn't want him to accompany her.

He watched her go down the block. The children came up to her and felt her beautiful blue dress and looked more closely at her beautiful face.

She looked back at him only once. She looked happy that the children were so accepting of her and seemed to like her so much.

She walked around the corner with them. Even from here he could hear their laughter. It was silver on the sudden cool breeze. His hangover did not bother him so much now. He thought of the man she'd had to sleep with. He felt angry, and stupid that he felt angry.

He went back to find John T. Stoddard.

Chapter Ten

Sometimes he forgot the name of the town he was in. With the coming of streetcars and tall buildings, with the coming of large glass display windows and crowded sidewalks, towns all began to look alike.

He could not, standing at the hotel window and looking down at the street, recall the name of this town, for instance.

He puffed on his cigar and continued to watch late afternoon passengers board the streetcar.

He looked at his pocket watch.

He was supposed to meet Reynolds downstairs in five minutes.

He turned around and said, "I'm going to go downstairs to get some cigars. I'll come right back up."

"Do you want me to go with you?"

"No. I don't think Victor will bother me anymore today. We got through our meeting. He'll be with his Mexican woman and his booze. It's tomorrow I'm really going to need you."

Guild smiled at him. "You're not going to need me tonight?"

"Not after dinner. I'd appreciate it if you'd sit downstairs with me and help keep some of the reporters at bay."

"Sure."

"Then you can take off if you'd like."

"Fine."

He stared at Guild a moment. He was not the sort of man he could understand quickly. Stoddard never knew when he was going to irritate Guild; he never knew when Guild was going to take offense. He would be glad when it was all over, when Reynolds had done his job, and when he no longer needed men such as Guild for protection.

The streetcar rattled away now. He had been paying particular attention to a woman in a white picture hat. He still loved to look at women, even though the last three years he had suffered the embarrassing loss of his manliness when he'd actually been with them. He wondered what it was, disgust over his wife leaving him or just age, that slow creaking crawl to the grave he saw in so many men around him, closed off to all experience but making money. He felt tears in his throat as he looked out once again at the town. He wondered if this would be the sort of place he would die in—big and anonymous—and without even knowing its name.

He put the flocked curtain back in place and went over to where Guild played solitaire.

"I'll be going downstairs now."

"You all right?"

"Why wouldn't I be all right?"

"You look sort of strange."

"I didn't hire you to be my goddamn priest."

Guild sighed and turned over a red eight of hearts. "You can leave anytime, as far as I'm concerned."

He had succeeded in pissing off Guild again. He almost felt good about it. He liked to see Guild upset and squirming.

It was always pleasant to walk into a taproom. He liked the smell of smoke and the hubbub of laughter and conversation. He liked the boozy heat of arguments about politics and sports. He liked the barmaids he tried to pick up for later and the bartenders he tried to intimidate with his self-confidence and his tips. It was fun to see them jump.

This taproom was fashioned after those in Chicago, everything done in stained oak, with brass fixtures along the bar and a huge mural of a naughty vaudeville lady named Ruby Lee stretching across the back wall. He had actually spent a night with Ruby Lee once. She'd had enormous breasts and equally enormous feet. He'd never seen feet that size on a woman.

Reynolds was at a rear table. He sat alone, a shot glass and a schooner sitting untouched in front of him. He was in his early thirties but older looking because he was balding. He was thin and wore a drab three-piece brown suit. He had small hands and nervous fingers. There was a certain air of sadness about him. He was one of the best thieves in the Midwest.

Stoddard sat down. When the waitress came over, he ordered a bourbon. When the waiter left, he said, "Are you all set for tomorrow?"

There was so much noise in the taproom that Stoddard did not have to worry about being overheard.

"There's only one thing."

"What's that?"

"You sure Victor isn't going to figure it out and come for me?"

"How's he going to figure it out?"

"You think he's going to believe it?"

Stoddard shrugged. "Robberies happen all the time. I'll leave Guild in the back room guarding the cash. If Victor blames anybody, it will be Guild. He hates him."

"He could still figure it out."

"Not if we're careful."

David Reynolds looked around. "This Guild, is he tough?"

"Not as tough as he thinks."

"He going to give me any problems?"

"Not if you do what I tell you."

"Which is?"

"Shoot him."

"What?"

"You want to make this look convincing, don't you?"

"Jesus, Stoddard, I'm a thief, not a killer."

"I didn't say kill him."

"Jesus."

"In the arm, maybe. Or the shoulder."

"I don't know. I've never shot a man before."

Stoddard smiled. "Then it's probably the only thing you haven't done before." Stoddard tried to know things about everybody he worked with. "You've developed yourself quite a reputation. Even for a man in your line of work. You get in and out, and there's supposed to be no trouble."

"After this is all over, I have to live in this town."

"Meaning?"

"Meaning if there's violence, the police are going to be looking for the thief double hard."

Stoddard took out a cigar and lit it. The afternoon light was dying in the window. A pretty barmaid passed by just now. He did not want to be talking to this frightened little man.

"You might even enjoy it, Reynolds."

"I doubt it."

"Some men get accustomed to it."

"I'm a thief," he said again with a certain obstinate pride.

"I don't want to have to worry about you. You're getting a nice little nut for half an hour of work."

"I don't have any objections to the nut, Mr. Stoddard."

"Good. Then you'll do it?"

Reynolds smiled. "You're a cold son of a bitch."

"I just want to relax and have a quick drink here before I have to go back upstairs. And I can't relax if I think you're not going to do it right tomorrow."

"Oh, I'm going to do it right."

"You're going to shoot him?"

Reynolds hesitated only a moment. "I'm going to shoot him."

"Good, then. It's settled."

"You really are a cold son of a bitch, you know that?" Reynolds said. But his words were not without a certain harsh admiration.

Chapter Eleven

Victor Sovich said, "You want to come with me?"

The woman looked at him. "Where you have in mind?"

"The next town, wherever that is."

"My children?"

"Your mother's across town."

"I leave my children?"

"It's no life for them, believe me."

"But my children. I love them."

"We'd come back through here every three or four months. The Midwest is good for me. I'd have to come back through here anyway."

They were in bed. The sheets smelled of their sweat and their lovemaking and the wine they'd had just before. He sat propped up against the wall and took in the smells. He enjoyed them. In the window the light was dying. It had turned yellow and pink. Now it was purple dusk. Through the smashed window he could see the quarter-moon. He smiled to himself. She was going to go with him. Oh, she would protest and tell him what a good mother she was. They always did. They needed that dignity. There was no other way they could face what they were about to do. He knew they wouldn't last long. These women never did. There would come a night or afternoon, some idle moment when he was shaving or bathing or reading a magazine, when he would suddenly have had enough of her, and then he would want to see her no longer. Then he would not be able to endure her touch or look at her body, clothed or unclothed, ever again.

"You like Maria."

"She's cute."

"Couldn't we at least take Maria?"

"I'd like to. It just wouldn't be good for her."

"Bobby, then. Perhaps it would be more appropriate for a boy to travel."

"It wouldn't be good for him, either."

Now was her time to sulk. She rolled over in the bed, away from him. He put his hand on her warm back, feeling the graceful curve of it, how it so fetchingly gave way to her plump, tender buttocks and the magnificent sweep of her long legs.

"Don't," she said.

Now it was his turn to roll away.

He lay on his side, staring at the wall. He could see the dirty handprints the kids had left on it. He could smell where the cat shit in the corner. Maybe he didn't want to take her with him tomorrow after all.

He kept staring at the quarter-moon and wondering about tomorrow. The nigger. He hated niggers and he wasn't even sure why. Something happened to him when he fought colored men. Something even he was slightly afraid of. He never liked to feel out of control, but with niggers in the ring that was usually the way he felt, out of control.

He remembered the first time he'd killed one. How the crowd had become silent so abruptly, how the referee kept saying, "Goddammit, boy. Goddammit, you wake now, you hear?" But the nigger had been dead already. The way all niggers should be.

After the fight a reporter came back to his dressing room. The reporter kept asking him how he felt. He knew Stoddard would get angry if he said the wrong thing. There had been more than one hundred ring deaths in the past two years, and church groups were really protesting prizefights. He did not say anything stupid. His livelihood depended on his not saying anything stupid. He said instead the expected things. That he was sorry. That he hoped the boy's family would understand. That he would say a prayer for the boy, in fact.

By the second time he had killed a colored boy, it was something most desirable for him to do. And not only for Stoddard's sake, but for his own. He enjoyed killing.

She was crying now.

He said, "You're a good mother. It's not like you're deserting them."

"They're my children."

"We'll see them often. I promise."

"What would the priest think?"

He scowled. "The hell with the priest." He remembered watching his sister die from smallpox. How the priest hovered. How the priest swooned. How the priest talked about an afterlife as if he really believed in it. As if we weren't like cats and dogs and rats, animals that died and rotted. He had had no time for priests ever since.

She only cried all the more. "I suppose you would like me to give up my faith, too?"

He stayed on his side, looking at the quarter-moon.

It was always like this with them. They cried and then they got indignant and then they got angry. But they always came along.

Always.

Stephen Stoddard liked to walk the streets at dusk, just as the first fireflies appeared in parks and the electric lights appeared on the streets.

He passed from the downtown, with its barbershops and millinery stores and banks and jewelers and ice parlors, to an address he'd found in the newspaper.

Most cities these days had Evening Home Clubs, where young men could gather to discuss the issues of the day without consorting with the type of people you met in pumprooms and taverns.

He was most interested in discussing the gold standard, finding it the one topic that always provoked immediate and prolonged conversation.

Given the letter he carried in his suit coat, however, he wondered how able he would be to focus on a debate.

Now, as he walked, Stephen Stoddard shook his head. Incredibly the ex-Pinkerton he'd secretly hired a year ago had finally found Stephen's mother. She lived in Portland, Oregon, half a continent away, and in the ten years since he'd last seen her, she'd gone on to start a whole new family. According to the photograph the ex-Pinkerton had enclosed with the letter, his mother was now plump, gray-haired, and surrounded by children bobbing around her like apples in a barrel.

His mother. He remembered soft, slender fingers and sweet songs hummed in the darkness. He remembered bread baking in the oven and the wet, clean scent of her long auburn hair just after she'd washed it. He remembered the sunlight on the new bicycle she'd bought him and moonlight on the silver ice of the skating rink.

He remembered her tears, too, how he'd been unable to stop them and felt the lesser for being so unable. The harshness of those tears. The increasing frequency of those tears.

Then she'd been gone, and gone forever.

Why, he'd never been able to understand exactly, nor had his father been able or willing to explain.

Now he held in his possession a letter that promised to tell him. The letter had come the day before yesterday. He had still not opened it. He did not know if he was frightened or simply savoring this first word from his mother in all these years.

Whatever, each time his soft, slender fingers touched the envelope, they jumped away, as if stung or shocked.

There would be an appropriate time, an appropriate place, to open the letter.

Soon now, he told himself as he moved along the sidewalk in and out of the shadows cast by the streetlight.

Soon now.

Guild had to be careful with the stuff. Put too much on and he smelled too sweet. A little was all he needed.

As he stood fresh from his bath in new black trousers, Leo Guild looked at the way the flesh of his chest had started to sag some beneath the wiry salt-and-pepper hair.

As if the stuff would magically make him younger, he splashed on a generous amount of the bay rum he'd bought at the barbershop a few days earlier. He next combed his hair and then pulled on a newly laundered white boiled shirt.

Putting on a false grin so he could get a look at his teeth, Guild at the same time began patting his stomach. Even if his chest was starting to go, his stomach was pretty damn flat for a man his age. Pretty damn flat.

He went over and sat on the bed and pulled on clean white socks and then his black Texas boots.

He wanted a steak and some bourbon. Most especially he wanted the company of Clarise Watson.

He started thinking of the little girl. It was usually like this. Anytime he was about to have himself some fun, the little girl came to mind. A priest had explained to him that this was one way of continuing to punish himself. The little girl was always there to remind him of that day. Of his mistake. Of his guilt.

He went over and sat on the edge of the bed. He looked around the hotel room. He thought of all the men who had stayed in this room before him. Of their pleasures and of their shame, of their loneliness for families far away. It was as if this room was haunted by all of them, a jumble of ghostly voices and griefs, but no voice, no grief was any clearer than that of the little girl's. He had never given a name to her, even though during the course of the trial—Guild ultimately acquitted—he heard it daily. But a name made her real in a way he could not deal with. She would always be just "the little girl." It was easier that way, somehow.

He opened the door on the third knock. He carried his .44 along with him. When he saw who it was, he leveled the gun to point directly at the man's stomach.

Victor Sovich was once again dressed like an opera star, complete with cape. This time he'd even added a top hat and cane. He said, "What's that smell?"

Guild flushed. He felt like an eight-year-old discovered doing something terrible. Sovich was referring to the bay rum. Guild said, "Some goddamn man before me must have spilled a bottle of bay rum."

Sovich sniffed. Then he smirked. "That must be it, Guild. Some man before you must have spilled a bottle of bay rum." He seemed to take as much pleasure from mocking Guild as he had yesterday from beating him.

"What do you want, anyway?" Guild said.

"I wonder if you'd like to talk some business."

"What kind of business?"

Sovich said, "Why don't we go downstairs and have a drink?"

"You can tell me right here."

"Is it all right if I come in?"

"No."

"You're still mad about yesterday?"

Guild didn't say anything.

"It wasn't anything personal, Guild. It's just that you're working for Stoddard. You know how it is."

"Why are you working for Stoddard?"

"What?"

"You heard me. You keep saying he cheats you yet you keep right on coming back. There's only one way to explain that."

"And what would that be?" The smirk was back.

"He's got something on you. Something he could use against you with the law."

Now the smirk grew icy. "I'm going to assume Stoddard didn't tell you anything, that you had this notion yourself."

Guild just wanted Sovich out of his sight. "What kind of business do you want to talk about?"

"He's going to short-count me again. He'll take eighty percent and give me twenty percent. If I'm lucky."

"That's between you and Stoddard."

"He'll probably have you guard the gate money and the betting money."

"So?"

"So you could take it all and give it to me."

Guild hefted the .44 again. "Now why the hell would I do that?"

Just then an old man in a flannel robe came down from the bathroom. He smelled of hot water and sweat. It was much too hot for a flannel robe. He kept walking, but he gave them both a big blue-eyed stare.

After the old man passed down the hall, Sovich said, "You'd do it because I'd pay you to do it. Fifteen percent of what you take from Stoddard you keep."

"Maybe the fight won't be as successful as you two think. Some of these fights people just don't show up for."

"Oh, they'll show up for this one." He smirked again. This expression was slightly different from the others. It was colder. "White folks always show up when a nigger's going to get killed."

"You ever think it could go the other way?"

"I never think that at all. Because it's not going to."

"I won't do it."

"You could make yourself a lot of money."

"I could make you a lot of money, you mean. And that I'm against on principle."

"You're going to be old pretty soon, Guild. Principle won't get you jack shit then. You'll need money."

Guild waved the .44 at Sovich. "Go on. Get out of here."

"Fifteen percent, Guild. You could make yourself a lot of money."

Guild slammed the door, but not before Sovich had a chance to smile again.

Guild went and sat on the edge of the bed until it was time to leave. He thought of the little girl. He wondered what she'd be doing now if she'd lived. Getting ready for the fall and high school, he thought. That was how he measured her years. Where she'd be in school.

Ninth grade now.

But of course that wasn't going to happen.

He had seen to that.

Chapter Twelve

"Well," said Clarise Watson, "I was born in Illinois and I moved to Connecticut when I was twelve, where a white man was very much taken with me. He saw to it that I was educated and that I learned how to dress properly and that I had proper dental work. He was grooming me to work in his house, which meant, among other things, being his mistress. His wife was this very cold white-haired woman who was difficult for everybody to get along with, including her husband. I'm told that he'd had other mistresses before. She knew about them and would tease him with them. She would get one of the mistresses' undergarments and leave it under his pillow. Or a gift he had given his mistress would be on his desk in the morning. She was the one with all the money, and all the power, and she never wanted to let him forget it. Finally she would make him so nervous and anxious that he couldn't have sex with his mistress. He'd keep trying, but his wife leaving all these little hints would undo him. She took more pleasure in handling it this way than in just throwing the girls out. She liked humiliating him.

"As I said, I was told all this. When it was my turn—he liked his mistresses to have just turned sixteen—he took me by the hand and led me out to this guest house they kept down by a stream. He took me inside and took my clothes off one layer at a time. I've never seen a man more appreciative of a woman's body. He was crying, and it was with pleasure.

"He carried me over to the bed and set me down on it and started to kiss me, and then it happened. I had no idea what was going on. He just started making these funny noises in his chest and throat, and then his eyes sort of started bugging out. I tried to help him, but I didn't know what to do. I ran up to the mansion to get somebody to help, and I was so terrified that I didn't even care that I was naked. Then she saw me, his wife. She came running out of the house with a riding crop, and I kept screaming that her husband was dying. But instead of running down to the cabin to see if she could help him, she started beating me. She must have beaten me for fifteen minutes. Finally I just passed out. She had them put me in the barn, in the haymow. They were under strict orders not to help me in any way. I stayed there for four days. I had to drink from the same trough the horses did. I got the chills so badly one night that I had to steal a blanket from a horse who was cold, too. I never forgot the look in his eyes. He seemed to know what I was doing and forgave me for doing it.

"The husband didn't live. The wife went to my family and told them that if they wanted to continue to work for her they'd have to send me to the city to live. She wanted to force me into prostitution.

"My father and mother had fourteen children. They had to look at the greater good—the well-being of thirteen children versus one child. I'm sure my mother never got over it, but they sent me anyway. I never did go into prostitution. I became a decorator for rich people. I even married a white man, but he could never forgive me for being a 'high yellow' as he always called me. Whenever he got drunk he beat me. He couldn't forgive me for being part colored, and he couldn't forgive himself for loving me.

"By then my brother had started boxing. I left my husband and traveled around with my brother until Rooney gave him that drink and killed him. And all this led me here, to try to kill Rooney.

"I'm sort of a disreputable woman, wouldn't you say?"

She said she didn't mind if he had an after-dinner cigar, so as they strolled along the river, he smoked.

On the dark water, the reflections of yellow and white city lights shimmered. Ducks floated and quacked. Rowboaters angled downstream toward the rush and roar and silver splash of the dam.

A soft breeze flowed over the grassy banks. Fireflies flickered and died. Lost in bushes, and happy to be lost, lovers giggled. An earnest young man in a straw boater sat on a park bench with a bored young woman and tried to impress her with his ukulele playing. An old immigrant sat in rags, despondent, staring at the shimmering water.

They walked upstream past the boat dock and the icehouses and pavilion where church ladies were carting off the last of the picnic baskets from a social.

"Have you even wanted a life like theirs?" Clarise asked Guild.

"I'm not sure."

"You ever tried it?"

"Sort of, I suppose."

"Sort of?"

"It's not worth talking about."

"Were you married?"

"For a time."

"Were you happy?"

"That's the part that's not worth talking about."

"I see."

They walked some more. He finished his cigar, tossing the red eye of it into the black water.

Electric poles hummed and thrummed in the dark night along the graveled river road.

A white-nosed fawn stumbled out of undergrowth like a lost

child, standing dazed in a circle of moonlight. Clarise went over to it and fell to her knees and hugged it as if she had borne it, and Guild was moved enough that he, too, went over and knelt and began petting the frightened animal.

At last came the fawn's mother, a loose-fleshed animal that seemed, seeing them, both scared and angry. You could smell the night's heat on the mother, and fecal matter.

The fawn disappeared back into the undergrowth with its mother.

Clarise and Guild went on their way.

They walked another mile. The river angled gently east. At its widest point the moon made the surface pure silver. Laughter came sharply from upriver, like gunshots, as two rowboats oared away from them.

They walked over and sat in the long grass on a ragged clay cliff above a backwash.

Clarise picked sunflowers, tucking one behind her ear. The other sunflowers she twirled, tossing them finally into the water below.

He was afraid to kiss her, but he kissed her anyway and she seemed quite pleased about it.

As they lay in the long grass, they could hear night birds and roaming dogs and distant cows. Nearer by, they could hear the soft lap of water on the shore and the wooden creak of rowboat oars and a young man singing a soft song, presumably to his girl.

He was scarcely aware of where his moments with Clarise were leading so suddenly.

"I can't help the way I am," Clarise said. "I don't like most men, and it's been a long time for me."

"Will you roll me one of those?"
"Sure."
"A lady oughtn't smoke."
"I suppose not."
"But then a lady, a real lady, oughtn't do what I just did."
"Aren't we a little old for oughtn'ts?"

She laughed. "Speak for yourself."

He rolled the cigarettes and got them going red in the dark night. He gave her a cigarette and then lay down again with her. They'd put their clothes back on in case somebody came along.

"You seem like a troubled man, Guild."

He did not want to talk about the little girl and spoil everything for them. He said, "And you seem like a troubled woman."

They said nothing for a long time. They just listened to the soft lapping of water on the shore and the reedy sound of breeze through the long grasses.

"I enjoyed myself, Guild."

"So did I."

"I guess I don't care if you think I'm a whore or not."

"I don't."

"That's what most white people think of us."

"You want me to tell you what most white people think of me?"

She laughed again. "Look at that moon. You ever wonder what's going on up there, in the parts that look like continents?"

"Sure. I wonder about that a lot."

"Wouldn't it be funny if there were people up there and they were just like us?"

"No," Guild said. "I hope they're not. I hope they're very, very different."

"In what way?"

He sighed. "I hope they don't have politicians the way we do, and I hope they don't let people go hungry, and I hope they don't kill children."

He felt her shudder. "Kill children? That's a terrible thing to think of."

"Yes," Guild said. "It's the worst thing you can think of."

"Then stop thinking about it."

She drew him back to her then, and the wonderful softness and heat and moisture of her mouth pressed to his again.

Chapter Thirteen

"Another one?"

"Please."

"You're all alone tonight, Mr. Reynolds." The bar was small, a narrow walk-in just off Church Street. The smell of whiskey and sawdust and stale ham from the free lunch filtered through the air.

"Yes." He left it at that. He did not want to talk about Helen anymore, or her marriage two months ago to a bank clerk. Everything had been fine with Helen until she learned by accident that he was a thief. She still loved him enough that she had not turned him over to the law, but nothing since then had gone right for Reynolds. Nothing. There had been, for instance, an easy breaking-and-entry job in Milan, Illinois, two weeks ago. He'd been going in through the back window when the entire casement fell down on his head, knocking him out. The incident had very nearly been comic. He'd come to with time enough to get out of the empty house with its walls filled with expensive paintings, its drawers filled with money and silver. Then he had tried breaking into the liquor store over on Harcourt Street. Two steps in he'd noticed a copper walking past the back door, a looming shadow. A copper. He'd cased the job for a week. Coppers were not supposed to come by for twenty minutes. But for some reason one did this night. He'd been forced to flee with nothing. And it all started when Helen told him she was going to marry the boy she'd graduated eighth grade with.

"You going to see the fight tomorrow, Mr. Reynolds?" the bartender asked.

"Isn't everybody?" Reynolds tried to make a joke of it.

"Darn near, from what I hear. You have tickets?"

"I bought one today, matter of fact."

"You're lucky. I have to work."

"It'll be some fight."

"The colored guy's going to get killed. You've heard about Sovich, haven't you?"

"He's killed several colored boys, from what I gather."

"You gather right."

Reynolds eyed him. "You like prizefighting?"

"Sure. Don't you, Mr. Reynolds?" The bartender had sort of a high voice for somebody who was so chunky and had such massive hands.

"I don't know. I always think I'm going to like it, and then the blood starts flowing—" He shook his head. "I just don't know if I do or not."

"Well, tomorrow's going to be special."

It sure is, Reynolds thought. *I'm going to have to shoot somebody. And with the way things have been going, I'm going to kill him by accident.*

"Special? You mean Sovich?"

The bartender nodded, wiped out the inside of a schooner with his white towel. "Sure, Mr. Reynolds. It isn't likely a town this size is going to see him again."

Six customers came in through the front door. They were laughing and slapping each other on the back. One, very drunk, was singing. He sounded Swedish. He was off-key.

68

The bartender moved down the bar to serve them.

This was what Reynolds had wanted, anyway. Solitude. He liked to stand at a bar and think through his problems and plan his robberies.

Tonight he'd gone to an alley with the Navy Colt his old man had owned. He needed to practice firing. His ineptitude with firearms was obvious. People assumed because you were a good thief you were also good with a gun. In fact, most of the robbers Reynolds knew were peaceful men. They would rather give themselves up than be shot or shoot at somebody.

He agreed with Stoddard that the robbery would look more believable if somebody was shot. Victor Sovich was less likely to be suspicious.

But he wondered how it would feel, shooting a man like that. Just shooting him.

He had a few more drinks—thankfully, the bartender got to talking with the group that had just come in and left Reynolds alone—and then of course he started thinking about Helen again.

Things had been very, very good with Helen. They'd made a lot of plans, including a family and a cabin by a lake they could share with her cousin in Wisconsin. They were even talking about what parish they were going to belong to (Helen was partial to St. Michael's; he to All Saints), and then it just had all gone to hell. He wished he were better at crying. Being a small man, though, he'd carefully taught himself not to cry. He needed every vestige of manliness he could summon. But sometimes crying would feel good, and he knew it. To just goddamn sit down and bawl like a baby. He'd seen his old man do it in the last failing months of the old man's life, when the black lung had gotten especially bad and when he coughed up blood more and more. He could never have imagined the old man crying. But there he was in bed, with his wife holding him as if he were her child and not her husband, and he was bawling away without shame. The old man didn't have her faith in the afterlife. He thought we were just like road dogs, nothing but ribs and a skull left of you, and then not even that after a time.

"Why don't you have a drink on me, Mr. Reynolds?"

"Sure. What's the occasion?"

"The fight tomorrow. Those men down there rode all the way over from Chicago to see it. They say it's going to be one hell of a fight, and the colored guy's going to be lucky he doesn't get killed."

The bartender poured him a drink.

"You be sure and go now, Mr. Reynolds."

"Oh, I'll be sure. Don't worry about that."

He wished there was some way he could explain to this Guild that he was really sorry he had to shoot him.

"Well, you not only be there but you enjoy yourself, you hear now, Mr. Reynolds?"

Sometimes Reynolds suspected that the bartender fixed himself good, hard drinks when nobody was watching. You could see this in the way he walked after a certain hour.

"I'll try to enjoy myself," Reynolds said. "I'll do my damnedest."

"That's the spirit, Mr. Reynolds. That's the spirit."

Reynolds had two more drinks and then walked back to his sleeping room. He propped the window up with a book and stripped down to his shorts and lay on the bed and smoked a cigarette. The smoke was gray in the leaf-shadowed light from the street. He thought of Helen and going with her dressed up to mass every Sunday. Jesus, but how sweet that would have been. Then he thought of this Guild he had to shoot tomorrow. He was going to get him in the calf and make it fast. In the calf there wouldn't be any way he could go wrong. If he tried to shoot him in the arm, maybe he'd hit the chest. Then things could go very wrong.

He lay there finishing his cigarette and then they started, the tears. He had to keep them down because the man on the other side of the wall would hear them and tell everybody in the boardinghouse.

He lay on the bed in the leaf-shadowed light all curled up like a little kid. His thin body jerked and started with his silent tears. He tasted them in his throat and his mouth and his nose.

He kept thinking of Helen and how he still loved her and how he would always love her. All she'd asked was that he'd give up being a thief, and at first it had seemed easy, but after a few weeks he'd realized that that was all he knew and that working a time clock job was just never going to work.

He wondered now who he was crying for, himself or Helen. Probably both of them.

He had another cigarette. Gradually his tears stopped. He reached over to the nightstand and picked up the Navy Colt.

He pointed it at the wall and made a small popping sound with his mouth, imitating the sound a gun makes.

He wished it were tomorrow afternoon. He wished it were over with.

Chapter Fourteen

They started arriving early on Saturday morning. They came by train, stagecoach, buckboard, horse. They came in ones and twos and threes and whole families. They came from farms and factories and neighboring towns. The local newspaper would make note that one man had been four days traveling and had come better than two hundred miles. Many of them hit restaurants and hotels and the local YMCA, but the majority of them sought out taverns and pumprooms. This was the sort of occasion you started getting drunk for early in the day.

Out on the edge of town, where the bleachers had been set up and a large canvas ring was in the process of being erected, there were already more than three hundred fans who had come early for the best possible seats. It was not yet eight A.M., and two men had already been arrested for drunk and disorderly and another for indecent exposure, the result of taking a pee behind a tree without noticing the fact that a family was having a picnic nearby. The temperature was nearing ninety, the humidity oppressive. Many of the police wore the tan khaki of the auxiliary policeman.

These cops looked especially young, trying to swagger around with their hands on their nightsticks but not quite knowing how to do it without looking somewhat ridiculous. The pickets had arrived, too, ten ladies in crisp summer pastels bearing signs that read BOXING IS IMMORAL and WE ARE NOT ANIMALS. A reporter from Quincy spent an hour with them, making note of their various complaints and trying to hide his own delight over the fact that today he was finally going to see Victor Sovich fight.

Downtown at the train depot, all the taxis were taken up as well as the ten buggies the city had provided for the occasion. The latter were reserved for the gentry, the men who wore three-piece suits and derbies despite the heat, the ladies in lace and contempt. These people were dispatched to the small city's two best hotels, where they immediately proceeded to ruin the days of bellhops, desk clerks, serving maids, and other guests.

Even most of the people who claimed disinterest in the fight had to admit that the town had never seen anything like this. It was as if the place had been set upon by vandals. Every square inch of ground, it seemed, was being stood upon, sat upon, or claimed for later by somebody who'd come here to watch Victor Sovich. In three taverns downtown there were large photographs of Sovich behind the bar. As a joke, one man from Chicago got behind the bar and lighted a candle to Sovich, the way Catholics light candles to honor statues of saints. The prank got five solid minutes of applause from the crowd and free drinks from the bartender, who considered the man a real crowd pleaser and therefore good for business.

In the city park an additional contingent of churchwomen had gathered to decry fisticuffs in any form, but especially the form in which it was done for money.

Two more people got arrested, one for being with another man's wife, and the second for drunkenly believing he was Victor Sovich. For no reason anybody could understand, the man simply began punching his friend until said friend was unconscious and perhaps dead. He'd taken a bad, twisting fall, striking his head on the curbing on his way down.

It was not yet nine A.M.

Guild said, "I'm not sure yet."

He was having breakfast in the hotel restaurant with Clarise. She had just asked him where he would go when the fight was over. "How about you? Where are you going?"

She smiled. "I'm not sure yet, either."

"We're quite a pair."

The waiter came. He was sweaty and angry, his hair plastered in wet ringlets to his skull. It was hot in here. Management didn't want to open the windows because the black flies would get in.

"You're having a bad time of it, I take it," Guild said.

The waiter, who was probably close to Guild's age, said, "They kept warning us about the fight and how the crowd would be and all. I thought they were exaggerating."

"They weren't, huh?"

"Most of these people are drunk already."

Clarise looked around. "You know, Leo, I think he's right."

The waiter poured them more coffee. Its stream looked red in the morning sunlight.

"Well, by the end of the day, it'll be all over with."

"Yes," the waiter said with a certain theatrical flourish, "or I will be."

"Stoddard's going to make a lot of money," Clarise said.

"Stoddard and Sovich. I don't think Stoddard will be dumb enough to cheat him this time. I think Sovich would kill him if he tried."

Her small, beautiful mouth wrinkled into a frown. "As long as Rooney doesn't make anything."

"He gets so much per round. That's how these things work. If he can stay on his feet ten rounds he can make himself some nice money."

"Maybe he'll get killed."

Guild sighed and looked out at the room filled with stout men in suits and thick mustaches, at women in chenille dresses, at curtains that looked like golden waterfalls with sunlight blasting through them.

Guild said, "You've got to forget about Rooney."

"That isn't very easy."

"I'm not sure you'd want to see him get killed, anyway."

"Why not?"

"Because there's a difference between wanting somebody dead and actually seeing them dead. No matter how much you hate them, you always start to feel a little sorry for them."

"I take it you're talking about your bounty hunting now."

Guild shrugged. "I suppose. You track them a few months and take them in, and by then you start to wonder if they are really guilty and what's going to happen to them in prison and what's going to happen to their families while they're gone."

"I haven't met many people like you, Guild."

"I haven't met many people like you, either, Clarise."

"Is that a compliment?"

"Of course."

"I just wanted to make sure."

Guild reached over and put his hand on hers. "You know what you should do?"

"What?"

"Get on a train this morning and leave this town."

"Why?"

"So you can break your tie to Rooney."

"What tie?"

"Following him around, always waiting for something bad to happen to him. He's got you."

"Got me? What're you talking about?"

"You hate him so much you can't let go of him. It's like being in love with somebody. You can't let go of him then, either."

"I hope Sovich kills him."

"Given Sovich's record, I'd say that that's at least a possibility."

"I know how I sound, Guild. So hateful. It's not very Christian. But I can't help myself. My brother was a decent man."

"I'm sure he was."

She paused, stared out at the blue sky and the golden sunshine. "You really think I should get on a train?"

"Right now."

"And go where?"

"Anywhere you can start a life for yourself."

"But I'd always think about him. About Rooney, I mean."

"But maybe after a while you won't think about him so much." He looked down at the remnants of his over-easy eggs, sausage, and toast. With the last remaining slice of toast, he wiped up a long, juicy streak of egg yolk and jelly. It tasted wonderful. He finished this off with coffee. He picked up a toothpick and got to work.

Clarise stared down at her long, delicate hands. They looked dark against the white tablecloth. In the hard light you could see all the crumbs from breakfast on the cloth. They seemed the size of pennies.

"I'm scared," she said.

"Of what?"

"Of not knowing where to go or what to do. At least trailing Rooney around gives my life a shape."

"I still think you should take a train out right now."

"You wouldn't be trying to get rid of me, would you?"

The waiter interrupted, saying, "We are supposed to ask all customers if they would mind giving up their seats when they're done with breakfast. The crowd in the lobby is out on the sidewalk and around the block."

Guild shook his head. "No, I've got to be getting up to Stoddard's room, anyway."

Clarise nodded, dabbed daintily at her mouth with a blood-red cloth napkin, and then stood up. She looked wonderful again this morning in a blue silk dress with a brocaded top. "I'll see you out at the fight this afternoon."

"I still wish you were taking that train."

"Don't worry, Guild. I can't shoot Rooney or anyone. You've got my gun." She smiled at him with very white teeth.

He walked her out to the lobby. The place was worse than the waiter had said. Everybody was shoving. It was like being on board a sinking ship. He managed to kiss Clarise on the cheek. She vanished into the mob.

Chapter Fifteen

He had worked as a field hand until he was fifteen. Perhaps because of his ugliness, which was considerable, and perhaps because of his surliness, which was also considerable, the white people who ran the plantation had never considered using him in the house. His father and mother were in the house. His sisters and brothers were in the house. But not him. No, he went out into the sweltering fields, where they put the worst of them—as they defined the worst of them, anyway—those fit not for social skills or the subtle machinations of being a servant. He was fit only for stoop labor where his hands got bloody from pulling everything from turnips to cotton from the ground and where on a lucky day in the corn he might have sex with a young girl.

He broke his first jaw when he was fifteen. A white man had watched as Franklin Rooney had at first resisted and then given in to the taunts of another black boy. Rooney went up to him and broke the boy's jaw with a single punch. How the boy had wailed. How the boy had backed away, terrified.

By age seventeen Rooney was a fixture on an eastern "colored" circuit of boxers. While the whites scorned him, as whites always did, the advantage to being a fighter was that it earned respect from certain types of black people, especially those who inhabited the taverns and brothels of Rooney's choice. Men feared him and women adored him. Sometimes even white women came to watch him fight, and there was no mistaking what he saw in their soft blue eyes.

But early on Rooney knew that despite his cunning, stolid body, his deft right hand, and a certain amount of ring skill, he would never be major. He watched other fighters, black and white, work their way up, but somehow it never happened for him. He stayed on the "circuit," as folks called it, and watched as other men, lesser men, succeeded. He was told it was because he "just wasn't ready for it." He knew it because he was so ugly, the nose too splayed, the lips comically thick, the eyes seeming to pop from his head. People who followed the fights wanted their man to look, if not heroic, at least decent. No matter what he did, Rooney couldn't look good. He fussed with his hair, he grew a beard, he had his teeth worked on, he took to wearing a gray cutaway and matching top hat. It didn't matter. No matter what you did to Rooney's face, you couldn't alter it. It was the sort of face that, no matter how long you stared at it, you never quite got used to.

He beat Jackson in '88 and Salivar in '89. He even beat a Chilean named Estafen. He awakened one day and noticed how gray his hair was getting. A few weeks later, fighting a plump kid he should have had no problem with, he nearly got knocked out. It wasn't that the kid was so good. It was that Rooney was getting so bad. Strength, endurance, quickness—by the time he was age thirty they had all left him. And they would never come back.

Wifeless, even finding few prostitutes who were willing to welcome him into their beds, he spent his life trying to make some sense of forces he sensed but could not understand. Why had he been born not only colored but so ugly? Why were less gifted men promoted when he was not? Would he ever know anything remotely like a normal life? The other day, walking up the street, he'd noticed a small cottage surrounded by a picket fence. A man and woman had stood in the yard, hand in hand, watching a dazzling little blonde girl play with a calico dog. Rooney had almost been overcome by a feeling that started out envy but ended up sadness. Would he ever have a life like that? Ever?

"You know what we're looking for, Rooney."

"I know."

"We want a show."

Rooney nodded.

"A good show, Rooney."

Rooney nodded again.

"He hits you, you get up. Meanwhile, you hit him every chance you get."

"You ever see Carter anymore?"

"Not anymore." John T. Stoddard's eyes dropped, and Rooney wondered what was wrong.

"He head east?"

"I'm not sure where he headed. He—died," Stoddard replied.

"Died?"

"In the ring."

"Carter?"

"Had you seen him in a while?"

"Not for a while, no."

"He'd started to get old suddenly." Stoddard shook his head. "You know how it gets with fighters."

"Yeah. I know."

"He found this kid from Pennsylvania. This really strapping bastard."

"A kid killed him?"

"Nineteen. But a punch you just can't believe."

Rooney got up from the chair. The three of them were in a small room on the east edge of the raw board building adjacent to the ring. The room smelled of heat and tobacco. The building was a warehouse for a tobacco wholesaler. Rooney was already stripped to the waist because of the heat.

"Carter. Dead." Rooney shook his head. "He was a decent man for a—"

Stoddard grinned and turned to the man he called Guild. "He was going to say 'a decent man for a white man.' You see, Guild, they think of us what we think of them." He laughed in a booming way that revealed anxiety beneath.

Rooney kept pacing. "Victor still hates colored folks?"

"I'm afraid he does."

"What we ever do to him?"

"You know how Victor is." Stoddard tapped his skull to indicate he was crazy. "You go fifteen rounds with him, you could be sitting pretty, Rooney. Sitting very pretty."

"I go fifteen rounds with him, I could be dead is what I could be."

"Victor's not so young anymore."

"That why he killed a fighter just last spring?"

"To be honest, that guy wasn't much of a fighter. He really wasn't."

Stoddard looked over at Guild. There was some doubt in his expression. "Now you're not going to go out there and just lay down, are you, Rooney?"

"We have an agreement. I'm going to stick to that agreement. I'm going to do everything I can."

"I need at least twelve rounds."

"I need my head on my shoulders, too." Rooney allowed a certain belligerence to come into his voice.

Stoddard glanced over at Guild again, then back at Rooney. "Why don't you show me a little something?"

"I ain't in the mood."

"Just a little something, Rooney. So I know you're fit and all ready to go." He patted his stomach. "You've been putting on weight, boy."

"I'm gettin' old."

Stoddard smiled. "Old is going around. Like the flu. Everybody seems to be catching it."

Rooney finally relented and showed him a few things. He

showed him a few right hooks and a few right crosses and a few uppercuts. He stood in the sunny corner and fought his quick moving shadow. The shadow was not quite as black as Rooney.

When he finished, there was a sheen of sweat on his back and arms. He went over and sat on the edge of a chair. He was panting. As he had told Stoddard, he was getting old. He'd fought many one-hundred-round matches in his youth. Today he was up against two things—the loss of that youth and the unforgiving hands of Victor Sovich.

"You know something, Rooney?"

"What?"

"You look scared."

"I got a right to look scared."

"You're going to be fine."

"He hates us folks."

"Victor isn't exactly a spring chicken himself anymore."

"That's what you said. That don't necessarily convince me."

"I need a good show, Rooney. A damn good show. There's going to be a lot of people out there."

"Sure. A man who kills other men always gets a crowd."

Stoddard paused. "You're forgetting something, Rooney."

"What?"

"You killed a man, too."

"Not on purpose."

Stoddard smiled. "That story kind of hangs on."

"What story?"

"That you poisoned his drinking water before the fight."

"That's bull."

"It's what I hear."

"It's not the truth."

"You just put on a show today, Rooney. That's all I care about. The past is the past."

Rooney noticed how interested Guild seemed since the conversation had come round to the fighter Rooney was accused of poisoning.

"I won't look good if you don't look good," Stoddard said. "You just try and remember that, all right?"

"All right."

Stoddard came up. He looked as if he were going to pat Rooney on the back. But you could see in his eyes the distaste he felt for the boxer's sweating body. He brought his hand back to his suit coat and put it in a pocket.

Rooney said, "You tell Sovich not to kill me."

"I'll tell him, Rooney."

"You promise?"

"I promise."

"I ain't got nothing against him. He shouldn't have nothin' against me."

"I'll talk to him, Rooney. You can bet I will."

Rooney sighed. "Maybe I'll retire after this one."

Stoddard said, "That's something to think about, Rooney. That sure is something to think about."

He and Guild left soon after.

Rooney sat in the chair. There was a fly in the room. Every few minutes Rooney tried to slap it down. He had no luck.

He thought about the fighter he'd poisoned that time. The kid wasn't supposed to die. All Rooney had wanted was to slow him down enough to beat him good. Then the kid up and died.

Rooney got up and paced. The sweat was now chill on his back, even with the heat. He was thinking of picket fences and small thatched cottages. He was thinking of a good woman with wide hips and a real way with children.

But he knew better, Rooney did. He knew it wasn't going to happen for him. Ever.

He stared out the window at the first hundred or so fans who surrounded the large ring.

There was only one thing they'd come here to see today, and Rooney knew only too well what that was.

Chapter Sixteen

Twenty minutes later, inside the office where the gate receipts would be kept, John T. Stoddard handed Guild a Sharps and said, "I want you to shoot anybody who comes through that door during the fight."

"Somehow I don't think your permission is enough. To kill somebody, I mean."

"Anybody who tries to get through there is doing so for only one reason. To take the gate money."

The office was snug, with two oak rolltop desks on the east and west walls, a bookcase filled with leather-bound legal volumes, a map of Dakota Territory, and one wall lined with advertisements for various brands of pipes and smoking tobacco. Sunlight fell hot on the floor. In the corner Stephen Stoddard sat at a noisy typewriter filling up a white sheet of paper with black-lettered information. He wore a white straw boater. Inside his coat was a lump that had to be a gun.

"I'll keep the Sharps, but I'll be using it only as a last resort."

"I wouldn't put anything past Victor."

"He probably wouldn't put anything past you."

Stoddard surprised Guild by taking his gibe seriously. "That supposed to mean something?"

Stephen Stoddard turned away from the typewriter. He was curious about his father's reaction to Guild's harmless remark.

"I said, is that supposed to mean something?"

"No, it isn't."

"Then why'd you say it?"

"I was making a joke."

"I don't find it one damn bit funny."

"You could always get somebody else for this job."

"A little late, isn't it, Mr. Guild? Two goddamn hours before the first preliminary fight starts?"

"Dad, I really don't think he meant anything by that," Stephen Stoddard said. He wore a white shirt with a high, starched collar, red arm garters, and a white straw boater. His trousers were dark blue and his shoes white.

"Did I ask you, Stephen?"

"No, I suppose not but—"

"Then you keep your goddamn nose out of my business, you hear me?"

"But Dad, all I said was—"

Stoddard moved across the room with easy grace. He poked a plump pink finger in Stephen's face. "Out of my goddamn business, you understand me?"

Stephen managed to look more miserable than usual. He could not meet his father's gaze.

"You understand me?"

Stephen scarcely whispered, "Yes, sir."

"Now you come on with me and walk the grounds."

For the first time, a look of anger showed clearly on Stephen's face. "I'm going to stay here, Dad, with Guild."

"The hell you are."

"The hell I'm not."

"Don't you dare talk to me that way."

"That's just the way I'm talking, Dad. Just the way."

Stoddard glared at his son and began to sputter something but stopped himself.

His glare turned to Guild. "You'd better watch yourself, Guild. You'd better watch yourself pretty damn close."

Stoddard turned and was gone.

Stephen Stoddard could not meet Guild's eyes. He went back to the typewriter and began pounding away again.

Guild watched him. He knew it wasn't his place to say anything, but he didn't have any choice. "You don't owe him, son."

Stephen continued to type, his back to Guild. "It's none of your affair, Mr. Guild."

"I don't like to see people suffering."

"I'm not suffering."

"Sure you are, son. Sure you are."

Stephen turned around and faced Guild. "He's my father."

"I know he's your father. He's also a bastard, and he's particularly a bastard to you, his own son."

"He means well."

"The hell he does. Your father has never meant well in his life."

"You're suggesting what?"

"That you leave. Get a job of your own. Show him you won't take his abuse anymore."

"It would kill him."

"Because you left?"

"Yes."

Guild rubbed at his face and sighed. "Son, he doesn't care about you."

"I'm the only family he's got."

Guild sat down in the office chair. He angled it away from Stephen. He put his Texas boots up on the rolltop desk and took out a cigarette and lighted it.

"You're some kid."

Stephen was already back to his typing. "I don't want to talk about it anymore. If you don't mind, I mean."

Guild inhaled deeply. He watched the blue smoke emerge from

his mouth. He tried a couple of smoke rings. They almost worked, but not quite. "You want to stay here with me?"

"Why? You don't want me to stay?"

"Fine with me. As long as you know what you're getting into."

"What am I getting into?" Stephen asked this with just a hint of mockery in his voice.

"There's always some risk when you have this much money."

"I've been around this much money before."

"But we're isolated here. Thieves could get in and out—"

Stephen shook his head. The white straw boater jiggled some. "I'm ready for any eventuality, Mr. Guild." From inside his blue coat he took out a Colt .45. "After all, it's the family money at stake."

"I'm not sure it's 'family' money, son. A big part of it is supposed to belong to Victor."

"Oh, yes," Stephen said, almost as an afterthought. "Victor."

It was going to be a very long afternoon, Guild thought.

"God did not mean for us to mingle the races, even in fisticuffs!" the man shouted to passersby. "The Bible expressly forbids mingling in any way!"

He stood at the bottom of the bleachers, an open Bible in one hand and the skull of an ape in the other. "It is from the ape that the colored man is descended. But it is from God that we white men spring. Please, stop this travesty!"

His pockmarked face, his sunken, exhausted gaze, his thin red lips that seemed always to be trembling, lent him the visage of a man not only mad but perhaps dangerous, too. Even the most swaggering of fans walked wide of him, unsettled by his presence in some way they could not define.

And so he stood in his ministerial frock coat, crying out as he had cried out on street corners and on trains and stagecoaches and in mainstream churches; cried out to be heard; cried out so that he could share at least some of the burden of his hatred.

"Help me end this travesty!" he called. "Help me end this tragedy!"

They kept on walking wide of him.

Chapter Seventeen

The streetcar was so crowded the conductor had to keep asking people to move back, otherwise he wouldn't be able to steer.

Reynolds stood near the rear, somebody's elbow pressed against his rib, somebody's shoulder against his shoulder blades. A stout woman's huge picture hat covered half of his face.

When the streetcar finally stopped, he was glad for the two-block walk to the arena. His legs needed stretching and he needed fresh air. He also needed to calm himself. The closer the time came to the shooting, the more anxious he became. He wished he had not agreed to this job, but backing out was the sort of thing he just couldn't do. Word would get around, and then people would begin to wonder if he would back out on *them*.

He bought a ticket and entered the carnival-like arena. A furious rumbling shook the wooden bleachers, the effect of so many people talking, shouting, screaming, laughing, cursing. He sat down and bought peanuts from a vendor. He dropped the shells on the bleacher and crunched them with his shoe. He stared down into the empty ring.

He still wished he had not agreed to this.

"You think he's going to kill him?"

Reynolds was distracted from his thoughts. A petite woman in a pink summer dress and a white straw hat held down by a gauzy piece of pink chiffon stared at him.

"You think he's going to kill him?"

"Oh. The fight."

"Yes. The fight."

"Well, I don't know. I don't actually follow boxing all that carefully."

"Well, I do and I think he's going to kill him. Victor's going to kill the colored man, I mean."

"It'll probably be exciting."

He knew immediately that his style of response did not please the woman. She glared at him as if he were some kind of circus freak and then turned back to her female companion.

He wished he had not agreed to do this.

The woman was now whispering something about him to her companion. Her companion smiled.

Blushing, Reynolds stood up. Now was a good time to check out the office, figure a way in and a way out.

When he turned back to the woman to see if he might not have been imagining her whispered insults, he saw that they were now both smirking.

Suddenly he became self-conscious about the way he moved. He tried to be more purposeful in his motions.

God, he wished there were not so many people out here.

God, he wished it were not so hot out here.

God, he wished he had not agreed to do this.

She took a carriage from the hotel. She liked the smart way the sleek black horse in traces picked up and put down its shoed feet. She liked the smart way the driver cracked his whip just over the horse's back so that the animal wasn't hurt in any way.

She sat back on the tufted blue silk seat and watched the buildings of the business district give way to small frame houses and then to real mansions, with wide stone gates and windbreaks of firs offering privacy.

She was aware that the driver turned back every minute or so for a glance at her. He was smitten, obviously. But he was also leery. He was white and he obviously suspected that she was not. Still, he could not quit staring.

It was hot in the carriage. She fanned herself with a black, Spanish-style hand fan.

Images of her brother filled her mind.

When he was seven.

When he was nine.

When he was dead there in the ring.

The driver was staring at her again. "You all right, ma'am?"

"Yes, thank you."

"You look troubled."

She smiled. "I am troubled. I'm impressed that you were sensitive enough to notice."

The man flushed. "It's just your face—well, it's easy to see what's in your soul, is what I'm trying to say."

"So you believe in the soul?"

"Yes, ma'am."

"A lot of men don't."

"I was raised Methodist."

"That's odd."

"What is, ma'am?"

"So was I."

"Methodist?"

"Yes. And most people think we're all Baptists."

"'Us,' ma'am?"

"Yes. Us." She paused, giving her word all the dramatic power she could summon. "Coloreds."

She watched his eyes. She was not disappointed. He looked as if he'd just suffered a sharp kick to the stomach. "You're colored?"

"You mean you didn't guess?"

"No, ma'am." He sounded miserable.

"You wanted me, didn't you?"

"Ma'am?"

"You desired me, didn't you, until you found out I was colored?"

He turned his head back to the street.

She wasn't sure why she'd wanted to hurt him. It was just this need that came on her from time to time. She needed to feel someone else's hatred sometimes. It revived her, brought her in touch with herself again. The hatred of others was a definition of all the things she could never be, no matter how badly she might want to be. The hatred of others told her very definitely who and what she was.

She said, "I'm sorry I embarrassed you."

But he wouldn't turn around now. He would take her out to the boxing arena and deposit her and leave as soon as possible.

"I really am sorry," she said. "You seem like a decent man, and I shouldn't have hurt your feelings."

The horses stepped smartly forward.

The day was very hot.

She wondered if, in the end, she would have enough courage for what she had ahead of her.

"Do you plan on killing him, Mr. Sovich?"

The kid had red hair and freckles and wore a cheap, loud suit and spoke an octave higher whenever he got nervous, as now. The older reporters gathered in Victor Sovich's dressing room let the kid talk because he was kind of funny to watch.

"Son, that's not a decent thing to ask me." Victor Sovich winked at the older reporters. "I just go out there and do my job, and if the boy happens to fall and not get back up, there isn't much I can do about that, is there?"

"Do you regret killing those other colored people?"

"Now you're getting serious, aren't you?"

"Yes, sir."

Victor Sovich, bare chested and fitted out with fine leather gloves, smiled toward John T. Stoddard, who stood in the corner.

"There's only one type of question Mr. Stoddard has asked me not to answer."

"What kind is that, sir?"

"The serious kind."

Several of the older reporters laughed.

But the redheaded kid persisted. "Do you ever get scared?"

"Me?"

"Do you ever think maybe you could be the one who gets killed?"

Sovich offered the onlookers another wink. "Maybe you know something I don't, kid. You think I *should* be scared?"

"No, sir," the kid said, writing something on the tablet he held out before him. "I just wonder if it ever crossed your mind."

"Do you have any idea how many fights I've had?"

"No, sir."

"Do you have any idea how many of those fights I've won?"

"No, sir."

"Well, I've had one hundred two fights and I've won one hundred two fights. Now, does that sound like a reason for me to get scared?"

The kid gulped. He had a huge Adam's apple. "No, sir. I guess not."

John T. Stoddard nodded to Victor and left the dressing room. He hated Victor's swaggering before the press. Victor swaggered enough as it was.

He felt grateful for the heat and the crowd. The crowd was invigorating.

He walked the aisles between the bleachers, noting how everything was going smoothly, from the vendors to the ice tents. After the "robbery," he was going to have a great deal of money.

One thing remained. He needed to get his son out of the office. He did not want Stephen there when the shooting started.

He headed back for the office, and it was then he saw Reynolds.

John T. Stoddard knew immediately that he had made a terrible mistake counting on Reynolds. Severe dark rings encircled the lower part of the man's eyes. His entire body seemed to twitch.

John T. Stoddard watched as Reynolds went inside the office building, obviously preparing for the "robbery" later this afternoon.

The door opened and a tall, gray-haired man stood there. "Help you?"

Reynolds couldn't find his voice. "Uh, I was just wondering if there was a toilet in here."

"There are latrines outside."

"I just wondered if there was a toilet in here."

"Afraid we can't help you."

"All right. Thank you."

When the door closed, Reynolds fell back against the wall. His chest heaved. His head pounded.

Could he go through with it?

He heard footsteps coming up the stairs. He should run, hide. He should not be seen anywhere near this office.

But somehow he couldn't move. He tried, but he couldn't.

"Jesus Christ," a harsh voice said, and when he opened his eyes there was John T. Stoddard. "You're supposed to be a professional."

He swallowed, wanting to defend his honor. "I am a professional, Mr. Stoddard. A professional thief."

"It's too late for me to get somebody else. I've got to depend on you."

"Couldn't I just knock him out?"

"You knock Guild out? Don't be absurd. You'd never get that close." He shook his head. "Listen, you miserable little bastard. We had an agreement, and I expect you to stick to it. Do you understand?"

"I'm going to be all right."

"You should see yourself—"

"I'm going to show you that I've got a lot more grit than you think."

"—pasty white and dark little eyes, and your left hand keeps shaking and—"

Reynolds moved away from the wall. "I said I'm going to show you, Mr. Stoddard. I'm going to show you."

He wasn't sure what he was talking about and felt he was just babbling, but he was tired of Stoddard's scorn. That was for sure. So now he tried to make himself appear as strong as possible.

"You've got a gun?" Stoddard asked.

"Yes."

"It's loaded?"

"I'm not a child, Mr. Stoddard."

"It's loaded?"

"Yes, it's loaded."

"And you're ready?"

"I'm ready, Mr. Stoddard. Yes, I'm ready."

"Then don't let me down, Reynolds. Don't let me down."

"I won't."

"You promise?"

"I promise."

After leaving the building, Reynolds walked over to a latrine and started vomiting. The stuff was orange. He closed his eyes so he wouldn't have to see.

Behind him a hick voice said, "Whooee! Whatever that little guy is drinkin', I don't want no part of!"

Rough male laughter filled Reynolds's ears.

He lurched from the latrine and walked with as much dignity as he could muster back toward the bleachers.

Chapter Eighteen

The first money came in a steel box latched with a lock. A hefty man in a three-piece suit and a walrus mustache delivered it. Guild opened the door for him. The man stared down at Guild's .44. "That Stoddard, he don't trust nobody, does he?" the man said. He was laughing.

He brought the box into the office, walked over, and set it on the desk.

"This is Stoddard's son, Stephen," Guild said, hoping the man would take a hint and not insult the father in front of the son anymore. Guild couldn't help it; he felt sorry for the boy.

"Yeah, I met him," the man said.

Stephen Stoddard pulled a piece of paper from inside his coat. He dropped to his haunches and held the paper up to the steel box. The paper held the combination to the lock. Stephen worked quickly, deftly. In seconds the lock was open and he was throwing back the lid.

The man whistled. "Your old man is having a good day, kid."

The box was packed tight with greenbacks.

"This is the biggest haul I've ever seen around these parts," the man said.

Stephen slammed the lid and latched the box again. He carried it over to the corner and set it on a small desk.

"I'll be back in another hour or so with the next box. It's already half full." He snorted. "The way them yokels is streamin' in, it may not take another full hour."

He went to the door. "Your old man said we wasn't to be drinkin' no beer today. That still hold?"

"Yes, it does," Stephen said.

The man offered them a sour expression and left.

Guild went over to the rolltop desk where he'd been sitting. He put his feet up and laid the .44 in his lap. He took a five-cent cigar from his pocket and lighted it. He watched the way the blue smoke turned the golden dust motes silver.

Stephen went over and stood by the money box. He touched it as if it were the most precious thing he had ever seen.

"Both Dad and Victor are going to make out all right on this one," Stephen said. "This is the one they've both been waiting for."

Guild took a drag on his cigar. "I don't think you should be here."

"What?"

"You're not hired to be a guard. I am."

"You think I'm afraid?"

"No."

"You think I couldn't cut it if I had to?"

"No."

"Then why would you want to get rid of me?"

"Because I've got a funny feeling is all."

"What kind of funny feeling?"

"The kind of funny feeling this kind of money always gives me."

"I'm his son."

"I'm surprised he would want you here."

"Meaning exactly what, Leo?"

"Meaning if you were my boy, I'd want you out walking around the stands. Putting a good face on things for the public. I wouldn't want you anywhere near the money."

"Dad trusts me."

Guild didn't want to say what he thought: *Your dad doesn't care enough about you to move you out of the way.* Instead he said, "Anyplace in particular you'd want to settle?"

"Beg pardon?"

"Anyplace you been thinking of settling when the time comes?"

"I couldn't leave Dad."

"I mean if something happened and you had to leave your dad. Where would you settle?"

He seemed afraid to even speculate. "I've just never thought about it." But his quickly averted eyes said that he was lying.

"You ever seen the ocean at Atlantic City?"

"Yes."

"Beautiful, isn't it? And all those girls on the beach."

Softly Stephen said, "It's very nice."

"You ever seen Vermont in autumn? I've never seen anything like the leaves in the hills. Like they're on fire."

"No, I've never seen them."

"Or a dairy farm in New Hampshire? The grass gets so green that the black and white cows really stand out against it on a sunny day. And it's so peaceful in the shade—"

"What the hell are you trying to do?"

"Just passing the time."

"No, you're not."

Guild sighed. "If you were my boy, you wouldn't be guarding the money, and that's for goddamn sure." He was angry at the three of them—at Stoddard for using his son this way, at his son for being used, and at himself because he could not seem to let things lie where they were.

"I'm not your son and I'm tired of your running down my dad. I should tell him some of the things you've said."

He had pushed too far. He had lost the boy. He could not help the kid now because the kid wouldn't let him.

He said, "You should ask for a cut."

"What?"

"You should ask your old man for a percentage of the take."

"I know you're trying to help, Leo, and I appreciate it, but you're really talking crazy."

"You work hard, kid. You deserve a percentage. That way when you're finally ready to leave—"

"You're getting kind of one note."

Guild stared at him. "You deserve a life of your own, Stephen. You really do."

Stephen walked to the door. "I'm going to go get some lemonade. You want a glass?"

"That would be fine."

"Big glass or small glass?"

"Big glass."

"I know you're just trying to help."

"I don't seem to be doing a very good job."

"He isn't as bad as you claim."

"Maybe not."

"He's my father. He raised me."

"I know."

Stephen said, "I'm going to stay with him till he dies, Leo, and that's the way things are." He spoke with a quiet determination that was all the more convincing for its lack of bluster.

He nodded and left.

Chapter Nineteen

Her four-year-old son said, "You will go far away?"

"Not far away."

"You will go with Victor?"

"Yes."

"I don't like Victor."

"I know."

"Maria, she is scared."

"I know she is scared."

"And I'm scared, too."

"I will not go far away, and I will return often."

"You promise?"

"I promise."

They stood in the center of the living room. The place looked better than it had in months. Victor had given her money to fix the place up. There was a new yellow spread for the couch, and two of the windows were fixed with new panes of glass. Where there had been a picture of the Virgin there was now a photograph of Victor. He had asked for it to be this way. Teresa had brooded about this for several days. Something about the Virgin made Victor uncomfortable. When she'd asked him what, he'd said, "It makes you look like a cheap Mexican. All these religious things on the walls." But of course Victor made her uncomfortable about many things. He had struck her several times with exceeding force, and sometimes when his teeth nibbled on her during lovemaking he seemed to take undue pleasure from the pain he inflicted.

Now her mother appeared in the doorway.

Her son ran to the older woman and hugged his grandma's thigh. He began sobbing immediately. "She is going to go, Grandma. She is going to go."

"You be a good boy and go play outside," the grandmother said softly. She knelt down to wipe away the boy's tears. She kissed him tenderly on the cheek and then patted him on the bottom and sent him on his way outside.

In the doorway the boy looked back at his mother.

Teresa raised her hand and waved good-bye.

The boy stood staring at her as if it would be the last time he ever saw her.

"Go play," his grandmother said.

The boy vanished.

The grandmother was scarcely five feet tall. She had skin the color of coffee and eyes the color of a midnight sky. She wore a loose-fitting white dress and sandals. She came over and sat on the couch, careful not to wrinkle the new yellow spread when she sat down.

"I do not want you to go," she said.

"I have already told him I will."

"It does not matter, Teresa, what you told him."

"He is expecting me."

"Your children are expecting you."

"They love you. They will be happy you are around them."

"Can you imagine what the priest will say?"

"He will say nothing to me."

"Oh?"

"Victor does not believe in priests. He does not want me to see the priest."

"It's terrible what you do."

"It's not. I will lose my looks in a few years. Then I will have only regrets."

"I have had three daughters."

"Yes."

"And I should be thankful."

"Thankful, yes. For our good health."

"And for one other thing, too."

"What?"

There was craft and malice in the old woman's gaze. "Only one of them turned out to be a whore."

Teresa flushed. "You do not understand."

"You think I was not young once, Teresa, as you are young—and beautiful, as you are beautiful?"

"It is different in the modern world, Mama."

"He made you take down the picture of the Virgin?"

"Yes."

"And he does not want you to see a priest?"

"No, he does not want me to see a priest."

"And he wants you to leave your children?"

Teresa said nothing. She did not want to be called a whore again.

"Does this not tell you about the man, Teresa? About what is in this man's heart?"

"He's a good man."

"In bed he may be good. No other place."

"We will be back often."

"You don't really believe that. I can see the lie in your face, Teresa." She wrung her brown hands. "You are so stupid."

"He loves me."

The old woman scoffed. "He puts gaudy dresses on your back. He makes you promises. He puts his seed in you. These things are not love."

"He said we will live in a fine house in St. Louis."

"You are forgetting your cousin Donna."

At mention of the name, Teresa lowered her head. "He is not like the man Donna was with."

"Oh, no? And what makes him different, Teresa? What makes him different?"

"Victor is a man of honor."

"So was her man until he got tired of her. And do you remember what he did then?"

"Please. You know how I hate to talk about it."

"He threw fire in her face so that she would be in agony and no other man would ever want her. He could not even give her the rest of her life, a chance to live well without him. He would not even do this much for her. So he burned her."

"Please."

"Do you know how she lives today?"

"I know."

"She lives in the cellar of her parents' basement because she looks so horrible that no one can stand to set eyes on her."

"He is not like this."

"Oh, no. He is a most honorable man. He makes you take down the picture of the Virgin, and he persuades you to leave your children."

She got up and walked across the room to where Teresa sat in a chair. She slapped her very hard across the side of the face.

Teresa began sobbing.

"Because he puts his seed in you does not mean he loves you, Teresa."

The old woman shook her head sadly, then went out the door and down the steps to play with her grandchildren in the sunlight.

Chapter Twenty

The referee was a man named Macatee. Stoddard had requested a man named Simek but Simek was sick with gout.

Stoddard knew nothing about Macatee, whose first name was George, and this made him nervous. He stood inside Macatee's dressing room, watching a bluebottle fly perch at an angle on the windowsill.

Outside the open window four women in crisp summer dresses carried placards back and forth. Obviously they knew this was where Macatee was getting ready. They wanted him to understand their seriousness.

Stoddard tried a nervous smile. "You can't escape them these days. They're in every town with more than one hundred people."

"Oh, they're all right."

"They are?"

"Sure. They just don't like to see people get hurt. Nothing wrong with that, is there?"

Stoddard continued to smile. "I like to see men get hurt. When men get hurt, I have a good payday. So do you."

Macatee had been shining his black boots with a coarse-bristled brush. The room they were in was smaller than many closets. There was a chair, a bureau with a mirror, and a spittoon.

As they passed by the window this time, the ladies leaned in toward Macatee. One of them, a redhead in an emerald-green picture hat, waved.

Macatee waved back.

"You know her?" Stoddard said.

Macatee, a tense little man with freckles on a white bald head, nodded and said, "I should. She's my wife."

"You have a wife who protests boxing?"

"It's her right. Just as it's my right to referee."

"Oh, I'm glad I came over here, Mr. Macatee. To see you, I mean."

"You are?"

"I certainly am. Do you know how many people are going to be here today?"

"How many?"

"The estimate is four thousand now."

Macatee whistled. He took a cigar from his shirt pocket, ran a lucifer along the front of the bureau. "Four thousand. That's the biggest sporting event this town has ever seen."

"That's one of my concerns."

"What is?"

"That the event lives up to the billing."

Macatee looked at him with eyes as green as his wife's hat. "What are you trying to say, Mr. Stoddard?"

"They tell me you're a good referee."

"I try to be."

"But I wouldn't want you to be too good."

Macatee blew heavy cigar smoke in Stoddard's direction. The blue-tailed fly was noisy in the corner. "Wish I had a swatter," Macatee said. "That goddamn thing's driving me crazy."

"You ever hear of the Sorgenson fight?"

"Sorgenson?"

"Over in Omaha about four years ago. Hmmm. Four years ago exactly this summer."

"I think I've heard of it. But what about it?" Macatee went back to shining his boots with the brush. He wore a short-sleeve shirt. He might be a small man, but he had outsize biceps for his size.

"Sorgenson was supposed to knock out his opponent pretty early in the fight. Everybody expected it. But Sorgenson was so good that he put the other fellow to the canvas in the first round."

Macatee whistled again. He didn't look up from his brushing. "Guess I should pay more attention to this Sorgenson."

"That isn't the point of the story."

"Then what is?" He still didn't look up. He seemed fascinated with getting the oxfords to shine perfectly.

"It's what happened after the first round. Sorgenson ran back in the ring at the top of the second and really started hitting the other man. Knocked him down again. Knocked him down so hard that the referee got scared."

"It can get scary in there."

"The referee stopped the fight."

"Oh. I see."

"Maybe you don't. He stopped the fight and a riot started."

"A riot?"

"It was a hot day, just like today. There was a huge crowd, just like this one. One man was predicted to win, just as Victor is supposed to win today. But the crowd still wanted a match. They didn't want to see it end too soon. They rioted. They took over the town and made it impossible for decent people to be anywhere near them for the night."

For the first time Macatee stopped his brushing. He raised his very green eyes to Stoddard. "You don't want to see this stopped today?"

"Not too soon."

"What if the colored boy gets hurt real bad?"

"He knows what he's getting into."

Macatee studied Stoddard's face for a long minute. "That story wasn't true, was it, Mr. Stoddard? About Sorgenson?"

"It was meant to illustrate a point."

"But it's not true."

"Not strictly speaking."

"Meaning there was no Sorgenson?"

"No."

"And no Omaha fight?"

"Not exactly."

"And no riot?"

"No, no riot."

Macatee had inhaled on his cigar. He was still studying Stoddard. "You're worried I'm going to lose you money, aren't you?"

"Yes, Mr. Macatee, I am. Especially now that I know your wife is carrying a placard."

Macatee picked up the shoe brush once again. He returned to his polishing. "I'm not going to let him get killed."

"Meaning what exactly, Mr. Macatee?"

"Meaning I'll stop the fight before it goes too far."

"Afraid of your wife?"

Macatee tapped his bald head. "Afraid of my conscience. I don't want to be responsible for a man's death. Even if he's colored."

"Just because a man gets hurt real bad, that doesn't mean he's going to die or anything like it."

"I know you want a show, Mr. Stoddard, and I intend to help give you a show. Just not at the expense of a man's life."

"You'll stop the fight, then?"

"When it's appropriate. I'm going to keep watching the colored boy's face close. When he looks like he's had enough, I stop the fight."

"The colored fellow wants to make some money. Remember, he's getting paid for every round he can get through. He'd sure appreciate all the money he could earn."

"It's nice you're so concerned for him," Macatee said. "The colored fellow, I mean."

"There's no call to get sarcastic."

"The mayor's office hired me because they don't want the responsibility of a death on their hands. If they hadn't hired me, or someone else with my attitude, Mr. Stoddard, you wouldn't have gotten your permit. A boxer dying may be all in a day's work to you, but not to the mayor's office. You have a fellow die in a ring like that and the state newspaper starts to paint you as an uncivilized place, and once that starts then businesses get real nervous about settling in your town, and pretty soon, before you know it, you've become a little fork in the road again and nothing more."

"That crowd's going to get awful mad if they don't see a fight."

"In Houston, I hear a crowd took its money back."

Stoddard said, "I'm just asking you to be fair, Mr. Macatee."

"How about if his eyes roll back in his head? Is that a fair time to stop the fight, Mr. Stoddard?"

"Eyes rolling back don't always mean anything."

"How about if he starts strangling on his own blood from his mouth being cut up so bad inside? Is that a fair time to stop the fight, Mr. Stoddard?"

"He takes a little salt water, he'll be fine."

"Or how about if his arms start twitching because his nervous system has been damaged? Is that a fair time to stop the fight, Mr. Stoddard?"

"He could be just arm-tired."

Macatee put the shoe brush down and dropped his leg from the chair. He stood up straight, touching a hand to a crick in his back. "I'm sure glad you're not going to be referee, Mr. Stoddard. You know that?"

Stoddard slid the white envelope from his pocket. He dropped it on the chair. "I like to give referees a little bonus. Before the fight."

Macatee stared down at the envelope. He leaned over and

picked it up. He hefted it, estimating the number of bills inside. He handed it back unopened to Stoddard. "I don't believe in bonuses, Mr. Stoddard. Especially before a fight."

A minute later, after stuffing the envelope back inside his pocket, Stoddard was gone.

Chapter Twenty-One

He went over to one of the thirty different beer tents. He knew it was the last place he should go.

He had a sausage sandwich and two mugs of beer. He figured that the food would help offset any damage the beer would do.

He hated it out here. It was too hot, the sunlight almost a bleached white, and too dusty. The dust smudged his clothes and got in his eyes and even down his throat.

He was eager now to get it over with.

He would go in and not even hesitate. He would shoot Guild right in the leg. When Guild was trying to recover, he would grab the money and flee. He would vanish into the crowd. That was the reason Stoddard had hired him. He was no good as a gunnie, but he was very good at vanishing.

So that not even Victor Sovich could find him.

He stood in the beer tent, hearing the first of the preliminary bouts announced.

A few more hours, he figured. A few more goddamned hours.

* * *

"I'm sorry I got so pissy."

"It's fine, son. We all get pissy."

"I know you're only trying to help."

"It isn't my business, and I shouldn't put my nose in it."

"It's just I wish you knew him better before you passed judgment on him."

"Maybe you're right. Maybe he's a wonderful man."

"You're being sarcastic, aren't you, Leo?"

"No, son, I'm not. Maybe he's a wonderful man and it's just my blind spot."

"He took right over as soon as my mother left."

Guild smiled at him. "He couldn't ask for a better son. You know that?"

Just then the crowd shouted and whistled and began stomping their feet.

"The prelim must have started," Stephen Stoddard said.

Guild picked up the rifle from where it stood next to the chair he was sitting in. He laid it across his lap. "Should be some more money coming our way pretty soon."

"I really am sorry I got so pissy, Leo. I hope you understand."

"Oh, I understand, son. I understand fine."

Stephen Stoddard grinned. "Maybe when this is all over, the three of us will go out and have some drinks. Would you go along if we asked you?"

"Sure."

Stephen Stoddard sat back and shook his head. "I've got a feeling you're good for him, Leo. He seems to act a little better when you're around."

"That's me," Leo Guild laughed. "A good influence on everybody I meet."

He rolled himself a smoke and checked out the rifle again.

Chapter Twenty-Two

They started rubbing Rooney with liniment half an hour before schedule. He was tightening up, and the bald, lanky man John T. Stoddard had appointed as Rooney's trainer could see why.

Rooney was obviously afraid he was going to die, and probably with good reason. Rooney, from everything Simpson, the trainer, could see, was no longer much of a fighter.

Oh, there had undoubtedly been a time when Rooney had been respected enough giving and taking in the ring, but he had probably always been one of those men who look more ferocious than they really are. Harold Simpson had been watching Rooney work out the past three days. If he were Rooney, he'd be afraid, too.

The liniment smelled of alcohol and another sharp odor. In the tiny dressing room the odor was overpowering.

"You probably should talk."

"Huh?" Rooney said, glancing up from his reverie.

"Talk. It would probably be good for you. You're real tight."

"I was remembering this fishing hole in Arkansas."

"Nice, huh?"

"Biggest snappers a man ever saw. And the water so blue and cold in the morning with steam coming up off the lake."

"Sounds pretty."

"Real pretty. Real pretty."

"You remember what I told you about his right hand. The son of a bitch comes up from nowhere."

But Rooney wasn't listening. "Then when it got hot you could lay back on the shore and look at the clouds. I never had it so peaceful before or since." Rooney was still back there fishing in Arkansas.

"You got to keep moving, first to your left, then to your right. It's your best chance, Rooney." He wanted to say your *only* chance, but he knew how that would sound.

"Sometimes I'd stay there right through the night," Rooney went on. "I'd get me a fire going by the shore, and I'd clean the snapper and put it in a pan and cook it right there. It was beautiful, the way the fire glowed in the darkness. Downright beautiful."

"You keep moving and his punches won't land clean. And if his punches don't land clean, he's going to get frustrated. And if he gets frustrated, you got a chance of hitting him back, Rooney."

Rooney turned his ebony torso toward Simpson. "You ain't been listening to me, have you?"

"You ain't been listening to me, either, Rooney."

"I was telling you about this fishing spot in Arkansas."

"And I was telling you about how to get out of that ring alive." Simpson said this with such vehemence that Rooney had no choice but to forget about Arkansas and face the situation at hand.

"I need to go fifteen rounds anyways," Rooney said. "I need the money bad, Simpson."

"He could hurt you a lot in fifteen rounds."

"Not if I keep moving like you said."

Simpson thought of the thick, ponderous body he'd seen working out yesterday. At some point in the past five years or so, Rooney had been hurt. The arms didn't come up quite right, the legs were always wobbly, and sometimes, for no reason, he'd start to shake.

Fifteen rounds could kill him for sure.

"You ever want to go with me?"

"Where, Rooney?"

"Back to Arkansas. That's where I'm going when this is all over."

"You are, huh?"

"Yes, I am. I'm getting me a pole and some elderberry wine and some good cigars, and I'm going to do nothing but fish for a month and watch the steam come up off the lake every morning."

"It sounds like it's going to be swell."

"It is. You wait and see."

Simpson had the impression that Rooney was gone again, was refusing to face the battle at hand by slipping into dreamy dialogue about fishing holes in Arkansas.

But suddenly Simpson knew better.

When he looked down at Rooney, he saw him starting to cry. "I'm scared, Harold. I'm scared."

Simpson put a white hand on the black shoulder. "It'll be all right, Rooney. You wait and see."

But Simpson knew better. Simpson was scared, too.

"This'll probably be the last big box," the guard said as he put the strongbox on the desk next to the other two strongboxes.

John T. Stoddard took the cigar from his mouth and nodded. Guild watched Stoddard as he obviously resisted the impulse to start running his hands through all the greenbacks.

Stephen Stoddard, standing next to his father, said, "Dad and Victor are certainly going to be on easy street after this one."

Guild said, "If this is the last big strongbox, why don't I take it all to the bank right now instead of letting it sit here the rest of the afternoon?"

John T. Stoddard turned and looked at him. "The agreement was that you'd guard the money, Mr. Guild."

"The agreement was," Guild said, "that I'd make sure your money was safe. It'd be a lot safer in a bank vault than here."

"You've got a rifle, don't you?"

"You know I do. You're looking at it."

"Then my money should be safe."

"The banker said we could bring it in anytime up till three o'clock. That gives us forty-five minutes. If we put the strongboxes on a buckboard, we could make it."

John T. Stoddard put the cigar back in his mouth and shook his head. "You ever do a job without offering your own opinion?"

"I'm not arguing with you. I'm just making a point."

"Well, you've made your point. Now I'm making my point. I want you to stay here with the money the rest of the afternoon while Stephen and I make sure everything's going all right in the grandstand."

"But Dad, I told Leo I'd stay with him."

"I want you to help me out, Stephen." John T. Stoddard seemed to make a point of being casual. But, watching him carefully, Guild saw that his eyes had begun to flicker anxiously. "Unless you've got a contrary opinion like our friend Guild here."

"I just thought I'd kind of help him out."

"I want you to help me out, Stephen. Do you understand that? I want you to help me out, and I don't want any more goddamn back talk about it."

Stoddard's attempt at casualness was now gone.

The office crackled with his anger.

Stephen went over and sat on the edge of the desk. He put his head down and said, "Yes, sir."

But his father wasn't done yet. "I'm getting good and sick of having to tell you everything. You know that?"

Stephen was shrinking into himself. "Yes, sir."

John T. Stoddard obviously needed to unload his formidable temper. He went over by the strongbox and slammed his fist on the desk. He whirled suddenly and jabbed his finger in Stephen's face. "The next time I tell you to do something, I want you to do it, and no back talk."

"Yes, sir."

"Now you stand up and precede me out of this office"

"Yes, sir."

Guild couldn't watch any longer.

Stephen would never be free of his father. Never.

Stephen glanced over at Guild. He looked ashamed of himself and ashamed of his father. He put his head down and walked out the door.

When the kid was gone, Guild said, "I think you finally got to him, Stoddard."

"Meaning what?"

"Meaning that I think you finally broke him."

"Did I ask your opinion?"

Guild stood up. He wanted to smash in Stoddard's face. "You want to keep him a little boy, don't you?"

Stoddard thumped the pocket watch in his vest. "In a few more hours, Mr. Guild, it is going to be my pleasure to pay you off and get you out of my life forever."

"I wish you'd do the same favor for your son."

"You just take good care of my money."

Guild said, "Something's going on, isn't it?"

"What the hell are you talking about?"

"There's a reason you're not letting me take this money to the bank, isn't there?"

"Are you calling me a liar?"

"No, Stoddard, I'm calling you a lot worse than that."

But Stoddard was already on his way out the door. "You'll be all finished in a couple hours, Mr. Guild. In the meantime, you just take care of the money."

After Stoddard slammed the door, Guild went over and locked it. Next he propped a chair under the doorknob so nobody could force his way in.

Finally he went over and sat directly in front of the door, his .44 in his lap.

He wasn't sure what John T. Stoddard was up to yet, but he now knew for sure that he hadn't hired Guild simply as a guard. He had hired Guild as some sort of patsy.

Chapter Twenty-Three

"I told her how you are about seeing women right before a fight."

"It's all right," Victor Sovich said to Kane, his pudgy trainer.

She stood in the doorway after Kane left. She looked crisp in her white dress, and beautiful. In her right hand was a suitcase.

Sovich smiled as she walked into the dressing room. "You did it, huh?"

"My mother is not happy."

"She'll survive."

"She says you'll get tired of me and throw me away. Or do something worse."

"You know how mothers are."

She came over and stood by the table he sat on. He had been rubbed down. He smelled harsh. The gloves had been put on his hands. "You seem so calm."

"I am calm."

"You don't ever get afraid?"

"What's to be afraid of?"

"Do you suppose you'll ever marry me?"

"I thought we were talking about boxing?"

"Is my mother right, Victor? Are you that kind of man?"

He brought her to him and put his face into her soft breasts. "I'm not exactly forcing you to go with me at gunpoint."

"Do you want me to go with you?"

"What did I tell you about the next time you asked me that? I said I wouldn't tell you anymore."

"Are you ashamed to tell me your feelings?"

He laughed. "No. But I am tired of repeating myself."

If he wouldn't repeat himself, she would repeat himself for him. "You told me you wanted me to go with you."

"If I said it, I must have meant it."

"You told me that I was beautiful and that you have never felt this way about any woman."

"I'm pretty good with the words, aren't I?"

"You said that if everything went all right that perhaps someday we would be married."

"Oh, I did, did I?"

"Yes."

"And how much did I have to drink?" He smiled and brought her tender body to his again.

"It was very hard saying good-bye to my children."

"I'll bet."

"They cried so hard I could hear them three blocks away."

"They'll get over it. You know how kids are."

"You don't care about them, do you?"

Just then his trainer knocked again. He held up a bottle. "This'll be your last drink before the fight."

He was happy for the chance not to get into the mess about her children. He held out his thick arm. "I could use some water."

He took the bottle and drank. The water tasted odd. He assumed it was from the well out here.

Finished, he handed the trainer back the bottle.

The trainer left.

Victor said, "Let's not talk anymore. Let me just hold you."

"You don't care about my children, do you?" she said. There were tears in her voice.

Victor sighed. "This isn't what I need right now. You understand?" He paused, then spread his arms for her. At first she would not come into the circle he made for her. She stood and stared like a frightened animal. Her tears made her seem much younger and quite vulnerable. Victor found this very erotic.

More softly he said, "Come here. Please."

"Will you say you love me?"

"Yes. If that's what you want me to say."

"I want you to say it because you want to say it."

Women were so simple, he told himself. All you had to do was shave and wear clean clothes and know when to tell them the right lies and they were yours.

So of course he told her that he loved her, and he told her that it was something that he wanted to say.

Her tears then were not of remorse but of gratitude. She thanked him in the same little-girl way she thanked him after they had made love.

But even as he held her, he was tiring of her. This would not be a long one. He liked them with some fight in them, and there was almost no fight left in her at all anymore.

Chapter Twenty-Four

The fight started at 3:43 that afternoon.

In all, 4,341 paying customers watched it. An additional one hundred policemen, army personnel from a nearby fort, and Mesquakie Indians from a reservation witnessed the bout.

In faces were pipes, cigarettes, cigars, and turdy lumps of chewing tobacco; in hands were soda pop, spafizzes, lemonade, and beer; on tongues were cheers for Sovich, curses for the colored man, and boos whenever the referee had the audacity to remind Sovich that there were, after all, rules to this contest.

It was ninety-four degrees when the fight started, and there was no wind. The latrines, filled with piss and feces, were rancid enough to spoil some people's enjoyment of the boxing match. The people in the confection tents worried that they would not have enough soda pop and beer to last the fight, particularly if the colored man surprised everybody and managed to stay upright for any length of time.

Occasional female faces dotted the crowd. These women generally fit into two classes—the girlfriends (as opposed to brides) of men who wanted to feel their girls were good sports, and the odd woman who had developed a genuine taste for the blood game. The former tended to squeal and bury their faces in a manly shoulder when things got nasty in the ring. The latter showed a silence and fascination stonier even than the men's.

The first round surprised everybody. Rooney did not do so badly. He did not do all that well, true, but he managed to avoid several uppercuts and to dance away from two hard right crosses Sovich tried to inflict on him. Once Rooney even managed to duck a bolo punch he saw only peripherally. Even the meanest of white men had to pay him begrudging respect for that one. If nothing else, Rooney's first-round performance implied that this might be, for a time anyway, something resembling a real boxing match rather than a carnival sideshow.

The second round immediately put the fight back in the sideshow category. Sovich threw three left hooks, each one of which caught Rooney square on the jaw. The second time he dipped to one knee and shook his wide, ugly head to clear it of cobwebs. With this, he brought the white crowd alive. They started yelling "Nigger," and when whites yelled "Nigger," the fight was only starting.

The third round was more even. Rooney landed two fair punches on Sovich's shoulders and one on Sovich's head. These blows did not seem to hurt Sovich especially, but they did infuriate him. Sovich had been hoping that the colored boy would have been set down for good by now. He rallied, of course, pasting Rooney with several powerful body shots, one of which lifted Rooney half an inch off the canvas.

By this time the temperature had risen to ninety-seven degrees.

In the fourth round, Sovich took complete command again. Two ringing shots to the head and three quick kidney punches once more brought Rooney to one knee. For the first time the referee began seriously evaluating Rooney's demeanor and behavior. He paid special attention to Rooney's eyes.

In the fifth round, Rooney shocked everyone, most especially himself, by slamming a roundhouse right to Sovich's forehead and pushing him back into the ropes, where he followed up with some solid but not spectacular body blows.

Sovich got out of the round, but barely.

"What the hell's going on in there, Victor?" John T. Stoddard asked in the corner while they waited for the next round to begin.

Sovich's entire torso was heaving. "Must be the heat."

"Do I need to remind you how much we've got riding on this?"

"You think he's going to beat me?" Sovich managed a smile that did not quite convince either himself or Stoddard of his skills at the moment.

"Forget about giving them a show. Just put him to the canvas. You understand?"

The bell rang.

"You understand?" Stoddard shouted into Sovich's ear.

"Yes," Victor Sovich said, spitting a mouthful of saliva and blood next to Stoddard's shoe. "Yes, you son of a bitch. I understand."

He rushed back to the center of the ring, determined to get the fight over with and soon.

Sovich felt angry. He liked it when he felt angry. Such a feeling always proved good for him and most unfortunate for his opponent. Especially if the opponent was colored.

At the top of the sixth, Sovich landed two smashing rights to Rooney's stomach. Rooney dropped backward to the canvas, landing on his bottom.

The white crowd shouted, screamed, cheered, and stamped its feet. They wanted to see one hell of a lot more of this kind of action.

The temperature was now ninety-eight degrees.

The fight continued.

Chapter Twenty-Five

Reynolds watched the first five rounds and then began working his way toward the office, making stops at a beer tent, a beef tent, and a foul-smelling latrine. Sweating had kept him sober, kept him intent on the plan that now seemed not only ingenious but inevitable. Just outside the office door where Guild sat, Reynolds would collect papers and rags and set a fire. There being only one way out, Guild would have to come to the door to find out what was going on. Reynolds would then shoot him in the arm, sneak in during all the confusion, grab as much money as possible, and escape. He had spent most of the past half hour looking at a route for himself that ran adjacent to a railroad bed running east. A fast creek ran below a small forest of poplar and pines, and he could easily wade into the water and move unseen downstream.

Now he was getting almost excited about using a gun.

He found the rags and paper he needed in a storeroom in the back of the office building. He soaked these in kerosene that was also conveniently stored in the same room and then proceeded up to the front of the building.

"Your father's going to have a nice payday, son."

"It sure looks that way."

"Though the fight isn't going exactly as he planned, I bet."

"No. I'd have thought Victor would have put Rooney away by now."

"You can't always tell with colored people." The gate man, one of the first people John T. Stoddard had hired in this town, touched his hand to the brim of his Stetson in a sort of half salute and then moved down the fencing to help out a man who looked both confused and irritated, standing half drunk in the heat and the hard white sunlight.

Stephen Stoddard turned back to the fight. At this point, midway in the ninth round, Rooney seemed as startled as any of the spectators. Not only was Victor Sovich not putting the black man to the canvas, he was beginning to lose the fight. Rooney had just delivered some slashing blows to the head and was now moving in with some heavy body punches.

The crowd did not know how to respond. It was as if a bishop had climbed into the ring and had begun singing dirty ditties.

It was very confusing. Rooney was supposed to be flat on his back at this point.

Stephen Stoddard wondered what Guild would make of all this. Guild usually had something interesting to say about nearly everything. Stephen decided to go tell him.

He wadded newspaper and rags into a single mass of flammable material and set it in front of the door.

He knelt next to it, taking a lucifer from his pocket as he did so. Calculating the direction the smoke would take, he pushed the material a little east of the door itself.

He struck the lucifer.

He sat back to wait for the smoke to start oozing beneath the door and for Guild to come out and see what was going on.

He had his gun drawn.

He was trembling so badly he had to hold his weapon steady with his other hand.

"What the hell you doing in there?" Victor's trainer shouted following the end of the ninth round.

"Heat," Sovich managed to say.

"Heat my ass. Your arms are dragging. You got to keep them up. You got to keep him from hitting you. That's the problem, Victor. He keeps hitting you, and you're not doing a goddamn thing about it."

The bell rang for the next round.

His trainer watched Sovich rise ponderously to his feet. He wavered, then wobbled as he put one glove on the ropes and started to walk to the center of the ring.

What the hell was going on here?

Guild, still seated at the rolltop desk with his feet up, thought he smelled something peculiar. Then he decided it was nothing more than all the combined odors, good and bad, of this afternoon.

The rags did not burn properly. Reynolds watched in frustration and anger as the flame reached the kerosene only to have it sputter out before any useful amount of smoke could be generated.

He snatched up the rags and ran back down the stairs to the storeroom for more kerosene.

The knock startled Guild, who had just been on the verge of falling asleep. He had started dreaming about the little girl he'd killed and was grateful to be awakened.

With his .44 in hand, he moved to the door and said, "Yes. Who is it?"

"Me. Stephen."

"I thought your old man didn't want you in here."

"You hear about the fight?"

Now that Guild listened, the crowd sounded almost surly. He wondered what was going on.

"Victor's losing."

"What?"

"Rooney seems to be getting stronger and Victor seems to be getting weaker."

"I'll be damned."

"Let me in, Leo. I brought some lemonade for both of us."

Guild shook his head and opened the door. He kept his .44 ready.

Stephen Stoddard stood in the open doorway with a pitcher of lemonade and two glasses.

"Figured you could use a break," Stephen said. "Probably gets pretty boring in here."

"I'm earning some decent money, kid. I don't mind it."

Stephen set down the pitcher and the glasses. He said ironically, "You changing your mind about my father?"

"Long as he pays me, I don't have any complaint."

Stephen sat down, poured them lemonade, and sat back in a squeaking office chair. "If Victor loses, my dad may be ruined."

"I'm sure he's been ruined before. He'll come back somehow."

"Not at his age." Stephen made a sour face. "There's just no way Victor should be losing."

"Maybe Rooney's a better boxer than we gave him credit for."

Stephen shook his head. "We watched him in three different towns, just to make sure he was the man we wanted. We figured he could give Victor a decent fight but he'd never win." He shook his head again. "Now look."

Guild sipped his lemonade and lighted a cigarette. He felt, as usual, pity for the kid and an inability to do anything about his pity. Maybe it would be for the best if the old man lost all his money. Maybe in doing so he'd have to cut the kid free.

Stephen said, "I told you about my mother."

Guild nodded.

"What I didn't tell you is that I hired this ex-Pinkerton to find her for me."

"Why now? After all these years?"

Stephen shrugged. "I suppose it's like a bad tooth, Leo. You never quit worrying about it."

"So did this ex-Pinkerton find her?"

"Yes."

"What's she doing?"

"Living her new life. Pretty happily, from what the detective said." He paused. Sorrow filled his eyes. "She's got a lot of new kids."

Guild sighed. "Makes you feel kind of bad, doesn't it? Knowing she started a new family and forgot about you?"

"Yes. Makes me wonder if she ever thinks about me or Dad at all."

"Maybe you should try to look her up sometime."

"She wrote me a letter."

"She did?"

"Yes."

"What'd it say?"

"I haven't read it yet."

"Why not?"

"Scared to, I guess."

"Probably be better if you'd read it, don't you think?"

"Maybe that's why I came back here."

"Why?"

"So I could read it in front of you. Maybe you could help me with it. Afterward, I mean. If I get real bad or something."

"Sure, kid."

"I don't want to hate her anymore, Leo. I'm tired of hating her. It takes too much out of me after all these years." He stared out the window. "Maybe she had a reason."

"Maybe she did." Gently, he said, "Why don't you open up the envelope?"

Stephen looked down at his hands and then brought his right hand to the inside of his coat. He took a plain white envelope from the pocket and set it on his knee.

"I'm kind of scared, Leo. I really am."

"You want me to read it to you?"

"Would you, Leo? Would you?"

Stephen sounded no more than eight.

"Sure." Guild reached out to take the envelope, and it was then he smelled the smoke.

This time Reynolds had gotten it going nicely. The smoke was an oily black snake slithering beneath the door.

On one knee now, his weapon aimed directly at the door, he waited for Guild to appear.

Leo Guild said, "Sit right there, Stephen, and don't move."

Guild handed him back the envelope unopened. "Afraid that's going to have to wait."

Guild took out his .44 and eased up to the door.

"What's the smell, Leo?"

"Kerosene smoke. Somebody wants to play a little trick on us."

"What kind of trick?"

All this time Guild was easing up to the door, flattening himself on one side of it so he could get a clean shot off when he opened it up.

"They want us to think there's a fire in the hallway. This gets me to open up the door, and then they come running in and take the money."

"Don't give them the money, Leo. Please."

"Just sit there, and let me handle it."

Guild was now up to the door. He dropped to his haunches and put a hand on the knob.

He flung the door open in a single motion, and that's when the firing started, as he had assumed it would. The bullets came at chest height, where he would normally have been if he hadn't ducked down.

The smoke was so thick Reynolds couldn't see anything. When the door opened, he fired by impulse.

Moments later he heard a harsh cry and then listened as a body slumped to the floor somewhere on the other side of the smoke.

Leo Guild turned just in time to see Stephen Stoddard fall from his chair to the floor. The bullets had gone so wild they'd taken the kid by accident.

Expecting more gunfire but hearing none, Guild crawled back along the floor to Stephen.

Even from here he could see there wasn't anything he could do for the kid. One of the bullets had entered through the forehead. The back of Stephen's head would look like a terrible purple flower suddenly in bloom.

Behind him he heard footsteps.

From the smoke emerged a short, slight man with a gun in his hand. He was coughing from the greasy smoke, and Guild saw no reason not to shoot him just because he was indisposed at the moment.

He shot him in the chest and the groin, and then he moved back up to the man's face. Just as the man began to crumple, he shot him in the forehead, right where the man had shot Stephen.

Standing, he walked to the front of the office and down into the smoke. Coughing himself now, he went down to the basement, where he found two water buckets. He filled them and carried them back upstairs. Putting out the fire was no problem. He put the smoldering rags and newspapers in one of the empty buckets and took everything back downstairs.

Back in the office, he got the kid propped up against a desk. He was still dead, but somehow he didn't look quite so vulnerable in this position.

He went back to the robber. He kicked the man twice hard in the ribs. He could hear bone cracking. The sound did not displease him.

Just then the crowd roared, and he realized that nobody had come running after the gunshots because most likely nobody had heard the shots. Not above the noise of the crowd.

He saw the white envelope on the floor near where Stephen had fallen from the chair.

He went over and picked it up. Red spatters of blood covered the front of it.

He wondered why she had left them. It seemed a terrible and incomprehensible thing to do. Maybe not to leave some son of a bitch as mean as John T. Stoddard but to leave the boy they'd raised together.

He folded the envelope twice and slid it down the back pocket of his black trousers.

He went back to the dead robber. He went through his coat and then his pants. For a time he was afraid he was not going to find what he was looking for.

But it was there, all right.

Oh, it was there.

He hunched there looking at the man's bad complexion. He stared at where the bullet had gone in the man's forehead.

He tried to tell himself the kid hadn't been happy alive, that maybe he would be happy dead.

He stood up and went over to the door and locked it securely behind him. Then he went looking for John T. Stoddard.

Chapter Twenty-Six

Victor Sovich went down for the first time midway through the eleventh round. What was so surprising for the crowd was that he was scarcely hit. Rooney had thrown a right hand, but it had glanced off Sovich's shoulder. It was not the sort of punch that could put a man down, but Sovich went to one knee, where he remained for a time while the referee counted off the seconds. Sovich, obviously dizzy, looked with dismay at his corner. What was going on here?

When he regained his feet and the fight went on, Sovich obviously made a decision—to throw his strongest punches against Rooney. The roundhouse, for example, was exactly the kind of punch that had killed people in the past, and probably would have this time—if it had landed. Still suffering from dizziness, Sovich threw three roundhouses during the remaining minutes of the round—but none connected, each missing Rooney's jaw by an inch or so.

The round concluded with Sovich wobbling his way back to his corner.

His trainer, trying to make some sense of what he was seeing, said, "You're letting him beat you, Victor."

"I don't feel well."

The trainer got angry. "Too much partying. Too many Mex women."

Sovich shook his head belligerently. "That water you gave me." He looked around for the water bottle. "It tasted funny."

"It isn't the water you should be worrying about. It's the partying you did last night."

Sovich scowled. "We'll settle this after the fight, you son of a bitch."

The bell rang.

"You'd better finish him this round, Victor. He's getting stronger and you're getting weaker."

Victor Sovich stood up on trembling legs and moved ponderously back into the ring.

The doc checked for vitals. He glanced up at Guild. Nothing.

The doc was a hefty man in a white boater and a yellow shirt and white trousers. He had come out here for a good time, and now he was spending his afternoon with a corpse. The doc, whose name was Fitzgerald, shook his head and got to his feet, his knees cracking as he did so.

He was about to say something to Guild, but just then the door crashed open and there stood John T. Stoddard. Guild had asked one of the boxing people to find him.

Stoddard's first reaction to being called back here was anger, then terror as he saw his son's pale hand on the floor from behind the table.

"My God," Stoddard said.

Guild looked away. He did not like Stoddard, but he did not want to take any pleasure in seeing the arrogant man's face begin to reflect the waiting sorrow.

Dr. Fitzgerald started to say something to Stoddard. "Be quiet," Stoddard said.

Stoddard's footsteps were heavy on the wooden floor. One,

two, three, four. He walked over and stood above his son.

"Who did this?"

"You know who did it."

Stoddard seemed shocked by Guild's harsh response.

"Reynolds did it," Guild said. "The man you hired to rob you. He wasn't much of a shot, Stoddard. Maybe you should have thought of that beforehand." He thought of what he'd found in Reynolds's pocket, the office key and a layout of the building. Only Stoddard could have given it to him. He smacked the key on the table.

Stoddard broke then.

He stood swaying miserably above his son, crystal tears on his jowly face. The sounds he made were intolerable for Guild to hear. Guild had sounded not unlike this one night shortly after the little girl's death.

Guild took Dr. Fitzgerald's arm and led him out to the hallway, where Reynolds was being wrapped in a blanket.

"What the hell's going on in there?" Dr. Fitzgerald demanded.

Guild shook his head. "He played it a little too cute, and it didn't work." He thought of Stephen. He slammed a fist into the wall.

"That's a good way to break some knuckles," Dr. Fitzgerald said.

But right now Guild didn't give a damn. He didn't give a damn at all.

Chapter Twenty-Seven

Sportswriters would later say that it was round twelve that proved decisive.

Rooney could scarcely believe what was happening. He started landing vicious body blows at will and then spent the second half of the round concentrating on Victor Sovich's face, opening up a wide cut above the right eye and even cutting him on the chin.

Sovich, so long accustomed to winning, began using almost pathetic defenses, limply putting his hands up in front of his face, only to have them smashed away by Rooney's blows.

For the second time in the fight, Sovich fell down. This time it was on both knees, not just one, and this time it was Sovich who had some difficulty getting back up. He knelt there, his wide white body sleek with sweat, one glove placed on the lowest rope as he struggled to regain his footing.

Fortunately for Sovich, the bell rang. His corner people rushed in and dragged him back to the corner.

* * *

"I didn't mean for it to happen this way," Stoddard said as they walked back into the office.

"Why the hell'd you have me come in here, anyway?"

"Because I want you to believe me."

"You want me to forgive you, Stoddard, and I can't do it. You set up the robbery so you could pretend to Victor that somebody else took his money. Only it didn't turn out so good."

Stoddard took some whiskey, stared down at the dead face of his son. "I treated him like hell, didn't I?"

"You know the answer to that."

Stoddard started sobbing. He put his face in his hands and wept.

Guild stood up and walked around. His boots were heavy on the floor. He went over, exasperated, and sat on the edge of the desk, where all the money was, and had a cigarette. He looked at the money and hated it as if it were a living thing. Then Guild remembered the letter.

He said, "He found your wife."

"What?"

"Awhile back he hired an ex-Pinkerton to look up your wife."

"What the hell are you talking about?"

"Here." Guild tossed him the envelope. "Stephen never opened it."

"Why not?"

"He said he was afraid to."

"He went to all that trouble, and he was afraid?" Stoddard's voice had started to rise in anger, the way it always did when Stephen had displeased his father. "I'm sorry. I shouldn't have taken that tone."

"It's the tone you always took with him."

"You want to hit me, don't you, Guild?"

"No."

"No?"

"Hitting you would be easy. You're going to have to live the rest of your life with how you treated him. That's going to be the hard part."

142

Something resembling a sob came from Stoddard. He lifted the flask and had another drink. "I wasn't always terrible to him."

"I know."

"I loved him."

"That's the hell of it."

"What is?"

"I really think you did. And you still treated him the way you did."

"It wasn't easy for me."

"I don't suppose it was."

"He never got over his mother leaving us, and I had to be both parents to him. Or try to be."

"Don't start feeling sorry for yourself, Stoddard. He's the one who died, not you."

Stoddard glanced up. "You going to tell Victor?"

"Right now I don't give a damn about Victor. I want you to give me my money, and I want to get out of here."

Stoddard brought his fist down on the desk. "I'm giving the orders around here."

"I want my money or I'll go and tell Victor myself what happened here."

Guild walked over and snapped his fingers and put his hand out. "I want my money right now."

But for the first time Stoddard was looking at the envelope on his lap.

Even before he opened the envelope, Stoddard was crying. Guild wasn't sure why, exactly. He just supposed Stoddard was a little bit insane now. Guild would have been.

Guild walked over to the desk with the money and started counting greenbacks. When he'd counted out his fee, he rolled the bills up and put them in his pocket.

Stoddard paid no attention.

He just kept reading the letter. He rocked back and forth and sobbed. Guild had seen Indian women mourn this way. It was not becoming to see it in a man.

Finished with the letter, Stoddard dropped it to the floor. He put his face in his hands and began his slow rocking again. He cried so violently Guild expected him to vomit.

Guild went over and picked up the letter from the floor and started reading it.

Chapter Twenty-Eight

Clarise sat in her hotel room, watching the street below for sight of the wagon that would take her to the train depot. She kept looking at the clock on the mahogany bureau. It was nearly five-thirty. The train left at six-thirty. She wanted to be certain not to miss it.

The heat, waning now, had left her feeling unclean. She hated that feeling. She rose and went over to the porcelain pitcher and basin on the bureau. Even warm, the water felt good on her face and hands. She opened her lacy blouse and massaged clean water onto the tops of her breasts. She thought of last night with Leo Guild. She had not liked a man, least of all a white man, in some time. But there was a humility about Guild she liked. That was the only word for it. Humility.

Going to the bed, she sat on the edge of the mattress, the box springs squeaking slightly beneath her weight. She looked at the yellow bowl of red apples against the light blue wall. In the sunlight the bowl and the apples and the wall looked like a painting. She stared at it until the tears came.

There should not be tears now, of course. She had waited so long for this day that she should feel nothing but joy.

The poison she had put in Victor Sovich's water bottle would be taking effect by now. His punches would be ineffectual. He would die in the ring, just as her brother had died in the ring.

At first Rooney would see this as a day for celebration. A mediocre boxing career would have been turned around. Rooney would have big plans.

The light in the room was the purple of dusk. In the street below was the clatter of buggies and wagons and the faint sound of laughter from the porch where oldsters passed the time by whittling on white wood and lying to each other about the past.

She wished her brother were here with her now. He would be pleased with what she had done.

A knock. "Taxi's here, miss."

"Thank you."

"He says shake a leg."

"I'll be right down."

"They like to have you there early for the train."

"Right down," she said again.

The room had enveloped her in melancholy, and she found herself reluctant to leave. The soft song of birds, the gray light in the window, the scent of perfume spilled in her carpetbag. She did not want to leave. If she closed her eyes she could be a little girl again. Her brother would not be dead and Guild—

She knew what Guild would think of what she had done. The words he would use.

She stood up, sighing.

She gathered her two carpetbags quickly and left the room, turning back only once to look for the last time on the peculiar half-light trapped in the corners of the place.

She wondered if death would be this soft and eerily beautiful. She hoped so, she hoped so.

"Hurry now, miss. Hurry now," the desk clerk said, looking her over again, still undecided if she was black or white.

Chapter Twenty-Nine

Portland

June 7, 1892

Dear Stephen,

When the detective came to my door, I was very frightened. I knew that at last my past had found me, the past I wonder about when I can't sleep at night.

If you have children of your own someday, you will know the particular hell I am describing, the hell of deserting your own flesh and blood. How many times over these past years have I wondered what you would look like as a young man. How many times have I heard the tears you surely cried when I left.

I know that no apology can undo what I did. I must accept my blame without any attempt at justifying myself. The worst thing I ever did was to desert my own son.

There is no point in castigating your father. I'm sure you

know by now how difficult he can be, and how he delights in belittling and bullying people. I can only say that I stood it as long as I could and then left. I should have taken you. I was afraid, however, that he would never rest if I took you, and he would someday find me, too.

The detective tells me that you work for your father and that you've grown into a healthy and handsome young man. When he saw me, he said that you still favor me. I suppose it sounds vain, but I'm glad you do. It's as if we still have a special bond between us, and the looks we share prove that bond.

Reading this over again, I see that your father was probably right—I was, and remain, a silly woman, spoiled by my own father and sheltered from the world in convent school. Even today I feel more like a girl than a woman, and when I look at the children I've had with my husband, Ralph, I feel a peculiar alienation—the same alienation I felt from your father and now my husband, Ralph. I know you won't believe this, but the only person I've ever felt close to—except to my father, who never had any time for me—was you. I think about you constantly. I hear a sentimental song and I think of the songs I used to hum to you when I rocked you in your cradle. I see a painting or a book—remembering how taken you were with paintings and books—and I want to buy it for you and send it to you.

I think it would spoil things if we met, Stephen. Tempting as it is, I think you would hate me the more for inflicting myself on you at this late date. And Ralph, to be truthful, would not understand. Long ago he tired of my tears and moods where you are concerned. He warned me that he would ask me to leave if I "moped" about you any longer.

At my age, darling, I can't afford to be on the street, and Ralph, handsome and rich as he is, would not think twice about putting me there. He is known to keep company with other women, and I assume at least a few of them would be more than happy to become his next wife.

But there I go, doing what I said I didn't want to—inflict my troubles on you.

I pray to sweet Jesus that you can someday find it in your heart to forgive me. I pray to sweet Jesus that someday I can forgive myself.

Love,

Your mother

Guild was outside the business office, smoking a cigarette, when the boy he'd sent as a runner came back with the fat, beer-smelling sheriff's deputies. Guild explained to them what had happened, carefully leaving out that John T. Stoddard himself had set up the robbery.

"His son got it, huh?"

"Yes."

"This doesn't look like Stoddard's day."

"Oh," Guild said, "what else?"

"The nigger."

"The fighter?"

"Yeah." The deputy wore a khaki uniform. Great dark circles of sweat ringed the areas beneath his arms. "He's winning."

"What?"

"He's knocked Sovich down four times now."

Something was wrong in the ring. Guild didn't know what, but Rooney had no chance against Sovich. None. "We'd better go tell Stoddard."

"Wasn't like Reynolds to carry a gun," the deputy said. "We all knew him. He was a robber, and a good one. But never carried any gun."

"He did this time."

"You have to kill him?"

Guild stared at the man. "Yes, I did, Deputy. I had to kill him."

The deputy shrugged. "Just asking." He nodded over to a

wagon. Two sleek black horses stood in traces. "We can use that to take the bodies back to town."

"Fine."

"I'll go make arrangements. Why don't you go tell Stoddard."

Guild nodded and went back inside the building. Dusk shadows filled the hallway now. Reynolds lay sprawled beneath a blood-soaked blanket. Guild stepped over him and went inside the office where Stoddard sat in a chair next to his son's body. Stoddard dumbly held a letter in his hand. Guild knew the letter was the one Stephen had been carrying but had been afraid to open. Stoddard stared down at Stephen.

"I don't know what to do, Guild."

"There's nothing to do," Guild said harshly. "You live with it, that's all."

"I didn't know he was going to die. I didn't want him to be here when Reynolds came in."

"Well, he was."

John T. Stoddard looked up. All the arrogance was gone from his face. He appeared to be a large, ponderous animal that had been wounded very badly. His eyes were red from crying. "You still don't like me, do you?"

"No."

"Can't you believe I'm sorry about this?"

"You're sorry for yourself, not for Stephen."

"I loved him."

"No, you didn't." He nodded to the letter. "Any more than she did."

"She didn't want to see him." He stared down at Stephen again and began sobbing. His great shoulders moved to the rhythms of his grief. He let the white letter fall to Stephen's chest. Red blood soaked it immediately. "He couldn't have asked for two worse parents."

Guild didn't say anything. He was tired of it all. He wanted to see that the kid was loaded on the wagon along with Reynolds, and then he wanted out of here.

The deputy appeared in the doorway. He glanced down at Stoddard and shook his head. He seemed disgusted with a man who would cry for any reason. He said, "You tell him about the nigger?"

"No, I didn't. Not yet."

"You better. Things are getting worse in there. Things are getting a lot worse."

Chapter Thirty

She watched him die. At first Teresa thought he was just having a bad time of it. She attributed this to the heat and all the food and liquor he'd had last night. The colored man was hurting Victor because of Victor's own excesses. For a few rounds she thought this might even be a good thing for Victor. Perhaps it would teach him some humility. Perhaps he would begin taking better care of himself and better care of her. Perhaps, though she knew this was very unlikely, perhaps he would even agree to take the children with them now.

Sitting in the front row, her head pained by all the hoarse shouting going on around her, she thought again of her mother's contempt and disgust. She had never seen such an expression on her mother's face nor heard such ugliness in her mother's voice.

The shouting got worse.

Teresa looked up just in time to see Victor get knocked down for the first time. It was then she knew he was going to die and that she could do nothing about it. It was more than just fear. It was some sense she had. As he was falling to the canvas, he turned his face so that he seemed to look right at her. She saw how vague his eyes had become, the way pain had wrinkled his mouth. Nothing broke his fall. Canvas and his head smashed together.

He got up. The crowd around her took this as a sign that the fight would turn back Victor's way. They shouted and clapped and stamped their feet. But she knew better, knew exactly what was going to happen to him.

You get used to being bad. You get used to seeing your once stone-fisted punches become as nothing against the face of your opponent. You get used to the feeling of strangling on your own blood from cuts inside your mouth, and you get used to the blindness that sets in after you've been hit so many times. When you get paid by the round, all you can hope is that you somehow manage to stay upright long enough to make good money for your day's work.

Today was different.

Today was the sort of day Rooney dreamed about when he'd had several schooners of beer and was sitting at a fishing hole. His punches were crisp and deadly once more. His opponent was driven to the canvas several times. Rooney, loose now with self-confidence and a real sense of how to take his man out, was once again a man others needed to fear.

He had lost count of how many times Sovich had pitched to the canvas by now. And it didn't matter. All that did matter was that Rooney was moving in slowly, cutting off the ring and making escape for Victor Sovich impossible.

He kept punching, punching.

She did not want to watch him die.

She sensed that even the crowd, that great roaring white beast that seemed to have its masculinity at stake here, knew he was going to die.

Its chanting fell to ragged silence.

Its boastfulness became soft curses.

Its anger became fear.

She took it as a sign from God. He did not want her to desert her children, and this was His way of letting her know.

She stood up just as Victor was knocked down for the fourth time. She was crying, quiet silver tears, as much for herself as for Victor, and she slipped from the arena without a single look back at the ring.

No, she did not want to see because seeing was a curse. If she saw him in his last moments, she would never be able to forget. In the night when it was hot and she could not sleep, she would see his dying face. Or in the winter when the hard winds came and woke her, then too she would see his dying face and her heart would turn bitter over things that might have been but, alas, were not.

She did not look back once. She went home to her children and her mother.

When he put his head down, the nigger hit him on top of the head. When he moved his body away, the nigger hit him in the kidney. When he fell to the canvas, the nigger hit him in the face on the way down. There was no escaping the nigger now.

Victor knew it was the water that had done this to him. But as the rounds pressed on, as the pain carried him into a kind of purgatory where all normal human reactions were suspended, he thought less about the water. Now there was just the blindness setting in, the sensation of pissing his pants, the right hand from nowhere inflicting more pain.

For a time he'd hoped that he could still turn the fight around. By now he knew better. As he bobbed and ducked and tried to retaliate, odd images began forming. He saw his father, Slavic-rough and Slavic-mean, tossing a baseball to a six-year-old Victor. He saw his sister Peg singing "Ave Maria" at Victor's first communion. He saw the first girl he'd ever slept with smiling at him knowingly in the shadows afterward.

More blows, abruptly. The referee, clamping his hands on Victor's face and forcing his eyes open, shouted right into Victor's face, "How are you feeling? Can you go on?"

Could he go on?

A nigger beating Victor Sovich?

Instinctively, Victor pushed the man aside and staggered in the direction of Rooney, swinging wildly as he did so.

The crowd roared for the first time in long minutes.

Rooney hit him very hard on the forehead again. Victor felt himself start to sink to his knees. A coldness came, then a darkness. He had experienced neither before.

His sister again, and the "Ave Maria."

His father slapped him for spilling too much beer in the bucket Victor always ran down and got him. (He'd never been able to please the old man. Never.)

The chewy breasts of Teresa. What an odd thing to want now with the coldness and the darkness setting in—sex.

The referee's hands on his shoulders, pushing him to the corner. "You're bleeding from your penis," the referee shouted into his face. "There's blood all over your legs."

He wanted, despite all the pain and confusion, to get Rooney.

And wanted Teresa, the musk of her sex, the soft brown sadness of her eyes.

Blindness was total now, and the coldness.

God, the coldness.

Chapter Thirty-One

The crowd was without voice. Where only minutes before it had urged its raging best on Victor Sovich, now it was nothing more than a whimpering beast, softly cursing its disbelief.

Dr. Fitzgerald was in the ring, bending over the unmoving form of Victor Sovich.

Rooney crouched on his haunches in the corner, keeping his massive, ugly head down, obviously trying not to pay any attention to the taunts and jeers directed at him by various white fans nearby. "He better not die, nigger. You hear that?" said one man as Guild pushed past to the ring.

The first drops of rain began to fall now, too, the sun disappearing altogether, the plump black rain clouds bringing not only darkness but chill, too. Rooney started rubbing himself. Seeing this, his trainer brought him a robe and threw it over his shoulders.

John T. Stoddard climbed up through the ropes. He was dazed

in such a way that his face looked dead, his mouth open, spittle a silver cord down the side of his jaw, his eyes shocked into a flat, unseeing blue.

"What happened here?" the trainer said to the referee as Stoddard wandered around looking lost.

"Rooney just came on strong."

"Bullshit."

"You asked me a question. I'm just telling you what happened."

"And I say bullshit. There's no way Rooney could have done this to Sovich."

"It's what happened. I'm telling you—it's what happened. The only thing I can think of is that Victor complained about the water."

"What water?"

"You gave him a bottle to drink from right before the fight. Maybe you still have the bottle."

"Back in the dressing room."

"Maybe we better have a look at it."

Stoddard came over now. The dazed look was still in his eyes. He stared dumbly down at Victor.

"He's dead," the referee said.

Stoddard said nothing.

"Dead, Mr. Stoddard. Dead."

The rain came harder now, cold and almost painful to the skin. The fans in the bleachers began to scatter. Where before there had been thousands, now there were only scores. Those who remained seemed not to notice the rain. They stood in their places, watching the ring.

Guild stared down at Sovich. He had not liked the man, did not like him still, yet there was an angry dignity to the man's Slavic face in the repose of death. His eyelids were cut badly and his nose had been broken and two of his front teeth were nothing more than stumps. His legs were covered with blood.

"Let's get his body back to the dressing room," Guild said to the trainer.

Guild got Sovich by the feet, the trainer by the shoulders. They eased him over onto a stretcher.

The referee said, "I've never had a man die on me before."

The sky opened up fully. The silver rain came in waves, in walls, in chill, shifting patterns that quickly drenched the parched ground beneath the bleachers and obscured everything in steam.

Somewhere in the middle of the downpour, they could hear an isolated fan shout toward the ring, "Is he dead?"

And the referee shouting back, "Yes, he's dead."

There was no sense in hurrying. Guild was already soaked. They carried Victor Sovich back on a stretcher covered by a sheet. The sheet got soaked immediately and clung tightly to Sovich, lending him the aspect of sculpture.

Guild tried not to think about the water bottle Victor had drunk from, but of course he had already begun to suspect what had happened. He thought of a woman whose brother had been given poison. Her brother had been a boxer, as had his killer.

They moved slowly back through the bleachers and along the rope fence and to the business office.

Guild said nothing. There was nothing to say.

Stoddard trailed along. He seemed barely able to pick up his feet. He said nothing.

They put Sovich on the rubdown couch. Dr. Fitzgerald checked him again. He shook his head.

The room smelled of liniment and trapped heat.

Guild got a cigarette going. He was watching John T. Stoddard sink into memories of his son when Sovich's trainer appeared holding a glass bottle half filled with water. "Here's what we're looking for."

Guild took the bottle and sniffed it. "Can't smell anything." He held it up to the light. "Looks clear."

"There are a number of poisons we can't detect right away," Dr. Fitzgerald said. "Not being able to see them or smell them doesn't mean anything." He looked at Stoddard heaped in the corner and said, "Mr. Stoddard, I'm going to pour you a glass of whiskey. I want you to drink it. Then I want you to get out of your wet clothes and lie down on that cot in the other room. Whether you know it or not, you're in a state of shock." He nodded for the trainer to help Mr. Stoddard into the other room.

Stoddard came suddenly and violently back to life. He jerked his arm away from the trainer's hand. "Mr. Guild here doesn't approve of me," he announced in a formal, almost theatrical way. He sounded as if he were right on the edge of tumbling into insanity. "He didn't think I was good enough for him, and he didn't think I was good enough for my son. He has a pretty goddamn high opinion of himself."

"Why don't you go in and lie down, Stoddard?" Guild said.

"Are you happy I'm ruined, Leo? Are you going to get drunk and tell all the men in the bar that John T. Stoddard is ruined?"

"Come on now," Dr. Fitzgerald said. "You go with the trainer and lie down and get a nap for yourself."

"He thinks it's funny," Stoddard said. "He thinks it's funny that I'm wiped out."

The tears were coming again. They were hard, bitter tears, and he might never recover from them. But they were better than his silence.

The trainer eased him out of the room and into the next. He got the door closed, but Guild could hear Stoddard's sobs.

Dr. Fitzgerald handed Guild a folded piece of paper. The faded bloodstains told Guild what it was. "Have you read this, Mr. Guild?"

"Yes."

"The poor kid."

"Yes."

Dr. Fitzgerald nodded to the door. "Is he really ruined?"

"I suppose."

"You don't like him, huh?"

"No."

"He's in a bad way."

"He deserves to be in a bad way."

"You're kind of a hard son of a bitch."

"You wouldn't say that if you knew how he'd treated the kid."

"Sometimes we treat people we love pretty badly."

"I guess so."

Dr. Fitzgerald looked at the door again. "No matter how much you hate him, Mr. Guild, right now he hates himself a whole lot worse."

The doctor's remarks cooled Guild's anger. Stoddard was probably not the villain Guild had turned him into. He was probably just as helpless and pathetic as Guild himself, living with his remorse over his son just as Guild lived with his remorse over the little girl.

The door from the hallway slammed open. A young man with freckles and a soaked gray suit stood there. "Didn't you hear it?" he said to Guild.

"Hear what?"

"The gunshot."

"Not above the rain."

"Somebody shot the nigger."

"Rooney?"

"Yeah. Rooney."

"Jesus," Guild said. "Jesus."

Chapter Thirty-Two

Guild recognized the man right away, the tall, frenzied man in the ministerial frock coat and the insane dark eyes. He sat in a corner. Reverend Feely. The fat deputy stood next to him. The deputy said, "In this town you're in trouble even if you shoot a colored."

"He killed a white man. Coloreds have gone far enough. Don't you agree?"

"Whether I agree or not don't matter none. They still put you behind bars in this town when you shoot somebody."

"Even a colored?"

"Even a colored."

"I tell you they've gone far enough, and we've got to put a stop to it."

"This is the gun you shot him with?"

"You think I'm ashamed of shooting him?"

"No. I s'pose not."

"And I ain't going to be ashamed when I go before a judge, neither."

Guild knocked on the door that led to the interior room being used for dressing. When the door opened, he stepped back so Dr. Fitzgerald could step inside first.

Rooney lay on the training cot. In his black face his white eyes bulged. Silver sweat stood in cold beads on his face. His big hands favored the massive hole in his chest.

His trainer said, "We got the guy, Rooney. Deputy's got him outside."

Rooney seemed not to hear. He just stared up at the ceiling with those bulging eyes. Guild wondered what he was thinking about.

Dr. Fitzgerald went over and started examining him. Once Rooney moaned, as if enduring intolerable pain. He started crying soon after. "I'm gonna die, ain't I, Doctor?"

"You're going to be fine."

"You're lying and you know it. I'm gonna die. I beat Sovich and a white man shoots me. It ain't fair."

"You lie there now and let me have a closer look at that wound."

"It ain't fair."

Guild watched Rooney's eyes. They were quick now with panic and fear.

As Dr. Fitzgerald bent over him, Rooney said, "They got a priest around here?"

"Lie still now. I don't think they have a priest."

"I got to tell somebody what I did." He writhed then with his pain. He was delivering death just as a birthing woman delivered life. Rooney looked over at Guild. "I poisoned this man, this nigger. He was a boxer. I shouldn't ought to done that. I just wanted to get ahead, was all. That was all."

His entire body jerked. His bulging eyes bulged even more. His body jerked again. His eyes closed, white eyes replaced by dark lids.

"He was lucky to make it this long," Dr. Fitzgerald said.

Chapter Thirty-Three

An hour and twenty-two minutes later, Guild stepped off the streetcar. His clothes were dry. He needed a shave. He was shaking and he wasn't sure why.

He stood on the street corner, letting well-dressed pedestrians swirl by him on their way to the opera house and the vaudeville parlor. He stared for a long time at the hotel. He wondered which floor she was on. He wondered if she'd left.

Dropping his hand instinctively to his .44, he crossed the street, waiting for a hansom cab to pass by, sleek and black in the streetlight. He liked the fresh smell of the city following the rain. It felt as though it had been purged of something foul.

In the lobby he went up to the desk. He asked the clerk if Clarise had checked out.

"No, she hasn't, sir."

"You're sure?"

"She was going to. Said she changed her mind."

"Thank you." He started away from the desk. "Oh. I need her room number."

"Four-oh-six," the clerk said without looking it up. His blue eyes said that he'd been smitten, and smitten most seriously by Clarise.

On the carpeted stairs Guild passed more people in evening dress going out. In his rumpled clothes, he seemed to elicit both amusement and disgust.

On the fourth floor he went down a long hall. At 406 he leaned forward to see if he could hear anything. Nothing.

He knocked.

Still he heard nothing. He glanced around the hallway and at the same time took his .44 from its holster. He tried the doorknob. Open.

He peered into the darkness of the room. Through a gauzy white curtain, plumped out from the window on a breeze, he saw a ghostly streetlight. The furnishings, bed, bureau, reading chair, and lamp were silhouetted against the glowing curtain.

He went inside.

The place smelled of Clarise's perfume. Despite himself, he allowed himself a moment's pleasure by closing his eyes and recalling last night by the river, the wonderful floating death of his orgasm and the fast roar of the water and the sweet, soft scent of her perfume.

She took one step from the shadows behind the door and quite skillfully got him square across the back of the head.

He was unconscious before he hit the floor.

"You figured it out, didn't you?"

"Yes."

"I don't want you to hate me, Leo."

"You killed two men tonight."

"Sovich has killed enough colored people. I don't worry about him. And you know what Rooney did. I wanted him to be blamed. I figured white folks would make his last minutes a lot more miserable than I could."

"A minister killed him. A crazy white man. But you knew a white man would kill him, didn't you?"

166

"That's what I was hoping. White folks don't like black folks who kill whites."

"You should have seen him, Clarise. There at the last."

"Did he suffer?"

"He suffered a lot. He was really scared, Clarise. The way you're going to be. The way I'm going to be."

"He killed my brother."

"I know."

"I tried to forgive him, Leo. I couldn't." She sighed and walked over to the window. In the street below, the clatter of hooves was sharp. "Back at the arena, I didn't think I could go through with it. I looked at him for the first time. Really looked at him. I saw that he was just human like the rest of us. You ever convince yourself somebody's not human and then all of a sudden you see they're a scared animal just like you?"

"All the time."

She turned back to Guild. She came over and sat on the edge of the bed. Her brown, gentle hands were folded in her lap. "I prayed God to forgive me, Leo, but somehow I couldn't warn Rooney. I wanted to. I wanted to get up and shout out that—"

She started crying.

Guild rolled himself a cigarette and watched her. He took two long drags, and then he got up and went over and sat next to her, taking her gently into the crook of his arm, putting her warm, wet cheek on his shoulder. Her whole body trembled.

"I wish I could feel good, Leo," she said. "I wish I could feel some satisfaction." She cried harder again. "I deserve what happens to me, Leo. I shouldn't have done it. I surely shouldn't have."

Guild walked over to the dresser. He took her bag and started throwing her things into it. He was neither gentle nor orderly.

"What are you doing?" she asked.

"You've got to go," he said. "Fast."

"But Leo, I killed a man this afternoon."

"He killed your brother."

"But I still didn't have any right to—"

"I said hurry."

Looking at him in a kind of shocked disbelief, she rose from the bed and moved like an uncertain child to the closet.

"Hurry," Guild said again.

She began taking dresses down from the closet and folding them in half. When she was finished, Guild took the dresses and put them inside the bag.

"Come on," he said.

"Where?"

"Depot."

"Depot?"

"There's a train pulling out of here in fifteen minutes."

"To where?"

"Does it matter? Now, come on."

Downstairs she paid the room clerk. He gave Guild, who was obviously nervous, a queer look.

In the street Guild kept her arm, steering her through the foot traffic and across the wide wagon-packed streets.

A block away they could hear the train getting ready to pull out. People's loud good-byes floated on the air like colorful balloons.

He made her sit as he bought her a one-way ticket at the counter.

On the way to the train, their footsteps loud on the wooden platform, she said, "You sure you should be doing this, Leo?"

"You let me worry about this."

At the car she boarded, she turned and said, "I wish we were going to be together again, Leo."

"It wouldn't work."

"Why?" she said.

Without humor, he replied, "We're too much alike. Now get on up there."

She started crying. "Leo, please, won't you reconsider? We could—"

"Board!" shouted the strolling conductor, checking his Ingram pocket watch. "Board!"

"You get up there," Guild said. "You get up there right now."

She leaned forward and kissed him quickly on the mouth.

He felt the kiss inside and out. He looked at her and felt alone. He wished there were some way she could stay.

"Board!" shouted the conductor.

The crowd pressed in, and she was lost in the midst of it, buoyed up the steps of the car as she moved inside with the others.

Guild knew better than to wait and wave.

He needed no more pain today.

Chapter Thirty-Four

In the morning Guild came down from his hotel room carrying his carpetbags. He had slept ten hours without any alcohol. Alcohol would just have made things worse.

He stood on the steps in the shade of the overhang. The bright day was already so hot the livery man down the street was sloshing water on horses.

From behind him a voice said, "I'd like to talk to you a minute."

Guild turned to find John T. Stoddard standing there, carrying carpetbags of his own. Guild said nothing to him, just turned away and started down the steps, heading for the railroad station where he'd taken Clarise yesterday.

As he walked, he heard Stoddard coming up behind him, panting, change jingling in his pockets.

"I'm sorry about the way I treated Stephen," Stoddard said. "If I could do it all over again—"

Guild set his bags down in the middle of the street and turned around and faced Stoddard. "I don't have any right to judge you,

Stoddard. I've done some pretty terrible things in my own life."
He frowned. "But don't ask me to forgive you, all right? That's
something I can't do."

"He liked you, Guild. Did he—" He paused, looking
aggrieved. "Did he ever say anything about me?"

"He said he loved you. He said that I didn't know anything
about your suffering and that I shouldn't judge you. That's
exactly what he said."

Guild picked up his bags and turned back in the direction of the
depot. He walked as fast as he could. He didn't want to see Stoddard ever again.

"Guild! Guild!" Stoddard shouted after him. "Please! Talk to
me, Guild! Talk to me!"

But then a streetcar came, and John T. Stoddard vanished
behind it. Not even his voice could be heard now, not even his
voice.